CALLIOPE AND THE ENGINE SMITH

Alex McGilvery

Calliope and the Engine Smith
Alex McGilvery
Cover Design by A.P. Fuchs
Zeppelin image © Philcold | Dreamstime.com

For information contact:
http://alexmcgilvery.com
ISBN: 978-1-989092-64-4

2

Chapter 1 Homecoming in a Strange Land

Cal stood at the rail of the Griffin and watched Lusundi slowly grow closer. The lush jungle contrasted with the misty greens of Anglia. She'd been to Lusundi before but never came home to it before. Roger's warm hand was the only thing keeping her knees from giving out.

"My father will be pleased to meet you." Roger squeezed her hand.

"Pleased to meet the woman who stole the third prince?"

"As I recall the decision was mutual."

"So what is a Congu wedding like?"

"It is a big party to celebrate what has already been decided between the couple." Roger laughed. "Lots of food and drink, gifts are given, and we dance. It is exhausting."

"I still wish we could stay and be part of it." Astrid came up beside them, her short blonde hair fluttered in the breeze. "But I don't want to bring assassins to the wedding. Gretta and I have decided to stay on until Ziyatha."

"Wise," Roger said, "but my father will regret missing the chance to meet you."

"It is too early to parade about." Gretta pushed a lock of dark hair behind her ear and poked Astrid. "We shouldn't even be here; someone might recognize us from shore."

"We must make our farewells here." Astrid hugged Cal and grinned wickedly at Roger. "You treat her right."

"We will go on a hunt after the wedding."

"That is the kind of thing we're talking about." Gretta poked Astrid again. "Let's get back to our cabin." They turned and went inside.

"Captain." Bundo stood still as a carving. "I may not accompany you in Congu."

"I'd rather you guard the girls." Calliope put a hand on his arm. "I can't be there, so be my right arm and keep them safe."

"I will." Bundo followed the girls.

"Hard to believe Astrid is the Crown Princess of Kershia." Calliope wiped at her eyes. "If anyone can turn the world on its head it will be her."

"We will see her again, I'm sure. It is hard to believe they are still schoolgirls." Roger smiled. "I'm not sure if you know about the Congu Right Arm, but they are warriors chosen for their loyalty and strength to guard royalty."

"Bundo is perfect for the job." Cal frowned. "I would rather he choose his own path, I will always be his captain, but I refuse to be his master."

The Griffin docked smoothly. Prince Roger and Calliope were the first off the ship.

"Roger." A tall man stepped out from a square of Congu warriors. Cal's back shivered when she saw the rifles in their hands.

"Bhansin." Roger embraced the man. "Good of you to meet me at the dock."

"The princess kkitatin insisted on returning to Lusundi to greet you."

The warriors shifted and a young girl in elegant gold robes which accentuated her black skin and fine bones walked over to Roger. Cal found it hard to judge her age, but from her height guessed at nine or ten.

"Father, welcome home." She glanced at Cal, but dismissed her, to focus on Roger.

Roger knelt to embrace the princess. "My Queen, I am home."

"Who is your guest?" the princess asked.

"She is not someone to be introduced on the dock."

"Welcome to Congu." The princess sent a calculated smile in Cal's direction. "Come, Father, the king is waiting for you."

The soldiers formed up around Cal, Roger and kkitatin and they walked into town and up the slope to King's Kraal. Cal sweated in the heat and was puffing by the time they reached the top. Kkitatin chattered the whole way explaining the sights to Cal as if they walked on level ground, not a steep hill.

The city was well built, with windows open to whatever breeze came by. Few were more than one story, but Roger had told her that many had several levels of basement.

They arrived at the courtyard of looked more like a sprawl of separate buildings than one. The guards waved them through.

A man, younger than Roger, stepped forward and took a place behind him. Chiza nodded at the man who nodded back.

They wound through confusing corridors to arrive at large double doors. The guards pulled them open so they could walk through without slowing.

"My king," kkitatin announced in a clear voice very different from her chatter. "My father returns." Cal was sure she'd heard an extra emphasis on father.

"Welcome, Son." The king was a much bigger man than Roger and covered with scars. He stood and walked to meet Roger, causing the people in the room to buzz with conversation. "You must tell us your hunt." He returned to his chair.

Stools appeared along with a table holding plates of fruit and water in heavy pottery.

Cal stepped back slightly to allow Roger and kkitatin to sit at the table. It would be her turn soon enough.

As Roger reported on his visit to Anglia, Cal took in the chamber. The king's chair was draped with brightly coloured cloth. Two younger men, sons of the King by their faces flanked him, standing easily.

The people in the room laughed or gasped at the right parts of his story. The tale of their visit to the Kershian embassy produced hearty laughter, but the king frowned slightly.

"And now I come to the woman by my side." Prince Roger took a deep breath. "I present to you Marquess Cal Shillingsworth, Admiral of the Air Navy of Anglia, and" he gulped, "my First Wife."

The room went still and every eye focused on Cal.

"Welcome, First Wife of my son." The King's eyes glinted "I can always count on you to surprise, Roger."

Cal nodded to him. A stool appeared for her, and she sat at the small table with Roger and kkitatin, who passed Cal a plate of fruit slices.

"My king, Cal has much to offer us but needs credibility in our country. As my wife, she has immediate status. I am going to ask my First Daughter to teach her our customs."

"You will need to take her on a hunt before the celebration, we want no challenges."

"My King," Cal's throat went dry, and she sipped at the water. "If you wish I will tell you my hunt."

"Interesting. I'm sure Roger has explained that simply killing game is not a hunt. The hunt tests our willingness to risk ourselves."

"I will tell you my hunt, and you can judge for yourself." She started with the days of drawing pictures for the scientist, then working with the engine. By the time she got to rescuing Pentam from the small sea serpent, the room was absolutely silent. She described building the steam cannon and how they lured the creature close enough to kill with the steam cannon. "I know it is custom to have some part of the hunt to show as proof," Cal grinned wryly, "but carrying around a tooth the size of my head would get tiring quickly. If you wish I can draw what I remember of the creature."

The king waved a hand, and paper and pencils were brought to her.

Drawing with the silent attention of the room was unnerving, when she was done, Cal stifled a sigh of relief and let a guard carry the drawing to the king.

"I believe this to be a true hunt." The king lifted the paper and handed it back to the guard. "Any who wish may look at this drawing."

***

Cal dressed in a simple dress kkitatin chose for her. A deep blue in the softest material she'd ever felt.

"It will show off your eyes." The girl insisted. "You need to be beautiful for my father." Speaking in Congu was a challenge, kkitatin had only a spattering of Anglian.

"And being pale makes that a challenge?"

"It makes you different, but my father has always chosen a different path." Kkitatin sighed. "It is my duty to support him."

"As First Daughter?"

"That too," Kkitatin said. "Did he tell you how I became his daughter?"

"He did, but I'm not sure I understand all the nuances." Cal didn't know the Congu word.

"I don't know this word *newants*."

"It means the little things that can make a big difference."

"Oh, like spice in a dish." Kkitatin's eyes widened.

"Very much."

Kkitatin pronounced Cal 'good enough' for her father, and they walked out to the throne room. Roger wore a robe with elaborate embroidery and applique on it in golds and blues. Maybe kkitatin knew the colours when she chose Cal's dress, but she felt very plain next to Roger's magnificence.

"Welcome." The king motioned her forward to stand beside Roger. There was some murmuring in the crowd packed in the arena, the only place large enough to hold all the guests. Fortunately, they had a tent set up for shade.

"A woman needs no adornment other than her own beauty." Roger spoke in Anglian, then in Congu.

"Will you let this woman hold your honour, and hunt with her by your side?" The King asked again in Anglian and Congu.

"I will." He smiled at Cal reassuringly.

"Will you hold my son's honour? Will you hunt with my son?"

"I will," Cal said in Congu and Roger's eyes twinkled at her.

"Then you will exchange names. Cal Hrona Xanichi Shillingsworth and Roger Shillingsworth Hrona Xanichi. Hold each other close."

Roger and Cal joined their hands.

"Time to feast!" the King called out to loud cheers.

Cal tried every dish, even the one with the honeyed locusts. They were all wonderful, some spicy enough to make her sweat, others cool and refreshing. People came by to congratulate them and leave gifts. Cal talked in Congu as much as she knew.

"If you were Sombi, people would expect you to speak your own language." Roger leaned over to whisper to her.

"I want to be Congu as much as I may."

"Appreciated."

"I was half expecting you to be wearing that yellow suit."

Roger laughed. "That would have set the tongues wagging."

"And an Anglian bride won't?"

"People are used to princes marrying outside the clan, it strengthens the clan. Given my history, they wouldn't be surprised by anything."

"Are you that different then?"

"Let's just say it took some adjustment to return to Congu from Anglia, I am meant to be a bridge between cultures. It is why father sent me to Anglia in the first place."

The feast ran down, and Roger carried kkitatin to her room.

"The tradition is for husband and wife to go on a hunt together."

"Then let us hunt."

They headed out into the dark jungle, Roger carrying a small pack.

"I hope I'm not expected to hunt in this dress." Cal ran her fingers along it. "It would be a pity to get stains on it."

"We have clothes to change into." Roger took her hand. "This is an auspicious spot." He set up a tiny shelter, little more than a tarp big enough to cover them both if they were holding each other very close. Cal laughed and hugged Roger tight.

"I said from the beginning this won't be a marriage of convenience or just politics." She kissed him. "We'll have to make it up as we go along because I have no idea what I'm doing.

***

Roger showed her the tracks in the jungle. "It isn't important what we hunt, only that we hunt together. I think it is meant to be a lesson about who we are. Cal wore a skirt with a length of fabric tied around her neck and chest. It was surprisingly comfortable. They followed dainty tracks in the soft earth of the jungle floor.

"Is there a creek or pond near here?"

"There is."

"Wouldn't that be a good place to wait, or are we supposed to track it down?"

"A hunt can be from a waiting place, or a chase, it might have people pushing game toward us. I think waiting at the watering-place would be a good omen. It is supposed to mean patience." Roger led her to where a tiny pool in a creek held many tracks in the mud.

"It would make sense to have one of us on the other side and one here." Cal stood still. "I remember my father talking about hunting on his trips, not just for specimens, but for food. "The breeze is coming from downstream, so if I wait here and you over there, shouldn't that work?"

"Let's try it and find out." Roger grinned at her.

Cal waited, trying to remember what her father had said about waiting without movement or fussing. She hadn't really noticed the insects until she tried to stay absolutely still. They crawled on her legs and under the cloth wrapping her torso. None of them bit her, or not very hard.

After a couple hours by the movement of the sun, but which felt like days, a delicate deer made its way hesitantly to the water. Let it drink, relax. As the deer lapped up the water it looked less like springs were wound tight in its limbs.

The deer lifted its head and looked around. It was now or the creature would be gone. Cal threw her spear like a harpoon. It passed through the animal's ribs.

"Well done." Roger stepped over the creek. "Clean, quick and no wasted meat."

"Do we have to go back right away?" Cal pulled her spear loose. "I get the feeling life won't be this relaxed for a long while."

"We can take a day or three if you want." Roger grinned at her.

***

"Kkitatin, what am to do with all this?" Cal stared at the mountain of gifts from plain to exquisitely beautiful.

"You must be seen to use them where possible. It honours the giver. In Sombi the gift would incur a debt depending on the honour of the giver and the status of the person receiving the gift." The princess shook her head. "I don't know what father was thinking making me your guide to our traditions, I barely know anything about Congu."

"I trust you will find a way." Cal wanted to pat the girl on the shoulder but wasn't sure if it would be appropriate.

"Shimah," kkitatin clapped her hands.

"Yes, First Daughter." The woman who came to stand beside kkitatin looked to be between the king and Roger in age.

"Beginning tomorrow, First Wife will be joining me for the lessons in etiquette."

"As you wish."

"Prince Roger." Announced one of the women.

"Good morning, Cal." Roger kissed her on the cheek. "And kkitatin."

The princess frowned slightly. "Good morning, father."

"What have I done to displease my Queen?" Roger sat at the table and picked up a comb studded with jewels.

"Should we not be First Wife and First Daughter?"

"You are more than those roles, when custom dictates I will use the honorifics, but otherwise I would prefer to address the whole of you." Roger put the comb down and picked up a tiny knife.

"As you wish, father." The frown didn't disappear.

"You may speak your mind, Daughter."

"I am still learning to be Congu, First Wife is just beginning, should we not act according to custom?"

Roger scrubbed his face with his hand. "Public custom is different from private custom. I hunted with the king this morning, what do you think he called me?"

"Would he not use Roger or Third Prince?"

"I think he may have called me Roger once or twice, mostly it was 'bloody fool'. I've been too long away from the hunt." He poured himself some water. "You are First Daughter, but you are also kkitatin, and my Queen, none of them address the entirety of who you are. We are more formal in the King's kraal, but even here we need to relax when we're alone."

"But we aren't alone."

"Do you trust your women?"

"Of course."

"They will not gossip about what we do in private."

"I will think about it." Kkitatin's frown deepened, then she flipped her hand and banished it. "When do we travel to your staal?"

"I was thinking of leaving in two days."

"As much as I want to show you the house I've prepared, we should stay at least another week. First Wife needs to show her appreciation for the gifts and meet with women."

"Good point, kkitatin. Shall we stay a week, will that give you the time you need?"

"It will, father."

The week passed in a whirlwind of visits and counter-visits. Cal worked hard on her Congu but had to rely heavily on kkitatin. Cal dressed to cover her skin - she'd had sunburn once - but fortunately, the Congu fashion suited her needs. Though kkitatin seemed to think Cal a living doll to dress as she wished.

Many of the women she met looked disappointed that she wasn't more outlandish, but Cal refrained for kkitatin's sake. She feared the girl's frown had become a permanent fixture. It only eased when Roger was able to join them. That wasn't often. The king put him to work sending messages to representatives from the other nations around them. There was a lot of suspicion about the idea of working together to deal with the Kershians, but they came around as Roger showed no ambition to rule, only to facilitate discussion.

***

Cal woke earlier than Roger, a rare occurrence. She called for a woman to help her dress for the day.

"I need to move around, please have someone come and escort me." Roger might not like the formality of the kraal, but he insisted that Cal never go anywhere unaccompanied by both a guard and maid.

They walked through the labyrinth hallways to a garden where she could relax and try to remember who Cal Shillingsworth was. The guard and the maid stood far away enough to give her space.

The first she knew of the attacker was a rough hand over her mouth. Cal bit down, hard and a rough hand slapped her. He hissed something at her in a language that was neither Congu nor Sombi.

If he wanted quiet then – "You dare?" Cal pulled on her commander's voice, able to be heard over the sound of running steam engines. The man winced and reached for her again, but she wasn't about to go meek and silent. She ranted at him, backing him into a corner.

When he reached for her, she slapped his hand away and increased volume.

Suddenly guards surrounded her, the man tried to run and met a spearpoint in the gut.

"Don't kill him!" Cal shouted in Congu. "The king will want to talk with him." The man wasn't moving; it was probably too late.

Roger arrived a few minutes later and scowled at the developing bruise on her face.

"What happened to the guard and maid?"

They found the maid on the far side of the garden lying bonelessly in a puddle of blood. The guard had vanished.

"Find him." Roger snarled at the men. They dashed off leaving Cal alone with Roger and the young man who had replaced Chiza as Roger's silent shadow.

"If he wanted me dead, I'd be a corpse." Cal swore under her breath. "I didn't recognize the language he spoke at me."

"What a mess." Roger put an arm around Cal. "You're shaking."

"As much anger as fear." She leaned her head against his chest. "I'm glad you're here." He guided her back to their suite.

"What happened?" kkitatin demanded. "Everyone in the kraal had to have heard that." She glowered at Cal.

"Later, kkitatin please arrange for tea and ask the healer to attend."

"Yes, father." She stomped off, but within minutes maids appeared to take Cal back to a room where an old woman prodded at Cal's face and peered into her eyes before grunting and walking out.

"I'm going to assume that is good news." Cal sipped at the tea the old woman had left. It was remarkably awful, but it settled the buzzing in her chest.

They didn't find the missing guard. Roger had a cold look on his face.

"He had to have been a traditionalist, upset that I brought home such a pale bride." He stalked off to speak to the king.

"You shrieked like a monkey." Kkitatin snarled at her. "Everyone in the kraal heard."

"That was the point," Cal said, too tired to soften the words. "If I'd been quiet, Roger would be looking for me now or planning my funeral. Use every weapon at your disposal, no matter how embarrassing, because that's better than being dead."

She walked away, angry at herself. The attacker deserved her rage; kkitatin didn't.

Chapter 2 Building an Elephant

Llathia stalked out of the cave and beat on a tree until her stick was splintered.

She'd heard rumours that the Anglian had flying ships, so had the king. At least he had more patience than her, but then he didn't need to prove himself daily to everyone around.

"Feel better?" First Wife looked like she'd come straight from the wives' quarters in the Kraal, not along a muddy, overgrown path between the temporary village and the cave. No one would guess from looking she was older than llathia's mother.

"It was the tree or Hovid, and it isn't his fault. As irritating as he is, he's also right." Llathia tossed the remains of the stick into the brush.

"What are people going to think when they hear the Mtuaka is breaking sticks against trees?"

"Probably be happy it isn't them instead of the tree."

First Wife laughed, the tinkle sounding odd in the jungle.

"There is a certain advantage to being unpredictable, but don't take it too far."

"I grew up with my father, I understand." Llathia straightened her shoulders. "You didn't come out here to defend the trees from my attack."

"The Third Prince returned from his hunt and brought a prize home with him." First Wife smiled slightly. "She is Anglian, and according to the rumours very interested in your engines."

"An Anglian? What did the King say?"

"Not much he could say but 'let's have a feast.'" First Wife frowned. "Word is that the First Daughter is not thrilled. I wouldn't be in her shoes. Her father comes home after months away, and she needs to share his time with a stranger."

"Poor kkitatin."

"Be careful, if you pity her, you will only make it worse. She needs to find her place."

"Right, message received." Llathia rubbed her temples. "He will want to visit his staal. I will need to talk with the steward about planning a suitable welcome. Better call it a day, then get back to the staal. Thank you for your kindness in visiting me with the news."

First Wife nodded slightly, then glided away back to the Engine Smith's village. Llathia walked back into the dim coolness of the cave. Eight men and women still stood around the engine.

"We have the task of making this thing fly." Llathia rapped on the engine with her knuckles. "Before it will fly, it needs to crawl. We need a way of moving it from one place to another, fire and all."

"Could use a wagon, but we'd have to lift it to get it on the wagon."

"Build one on the wagon."

"What's going to pull it? Horses can't manage it."

"Would need a special wagon too."

"Fine, build a wagon, then build a small engine on it. Then we'll figure out how to make it move. I must return to the staal.

Have the wagon and engine built and then we can decide on the next step."

"Yes, Engine Smith." Hovid crossed his arms. "We can do that."

"Hovid, I trust you make a wagon and an engine. The people you don't need for that will come up with a way to make the wagon move."

"The engine is as heavy as an elephant." Hovid's crossed arms tightened.

"You're right, but for now, it doesn't need to fly. As you know, elephants can walk."

***

When Llathia saw Chiza waiting for her, she forgot about the Anglian woman and ran into his arms.

"Oh, I've missed you." She said into his chest.

"And I you." They stood like that until her heart slowed its thumping.

"How was your hunt?"

"Interesting, I didn't think after all the years I've been with him that he could still surprise me."

"The Anglian woman? What's she like?"

"She is an Anglian engine smith. The Kershians abducted and tried to enslave her. She destroyed a mountain to escape. The Anglians made her nobility, but Cal worked in the engine room of the ship we travelled on."

"It sounds like she impressed you."

"Not near as much as you." Chiza squeezed her, then stepped back and took her hand. "They will be here in about a week. The princess wanted to show her off."

"I can imagine, she doesn't have many her own age to play with, it is like she was born an adult."

"What was she like here?"

"As long as there was something for her to do, she was great, but the slightest hint of boredom and the claws came out. Preparing the staal for the Third Prince kept her busy for a while, once it was finished, she made me happy enough to let her go to the kraal to wait for her father."

"Let's go get something to eat, then I need to start planning their welcome. Any advice?" Llathia stretched up on tip toe to kiss his lips.

"Be yourself, let the woman find her own place. She is First Wife of the Third Prince; you are the Lady Mtuaka."

"I still have trouble believing that."

"You will need to believe it."

Llathia took his hand and led him inside.

"Lady Mtuaka," Ndaax, her steward, met her at the door. "The villages along the river are complaining they are hungry. The young men are across the river fighting the Kershians."

"We've been over this. They may send people to help with the harvest around the Third Prince's staal. They keep a tenth of what they pick."

"They fear an attack from over the river." Ndaax looked down his nose at her.

"One doesn't need to be a warrior to dig roots."

"Very well, I will send the message again." He looked up at Chiza, then shrugged, saluted and walked away muttering.

"If he wasn't so useful, I'd feed him to the crocodiles."

"They are still fighting in Sombi?"

"Most of it is up here. The Kershians built a fort where their rail line was blocked. They want the black rock they burn in their engines. The young warriors just want to fight so they neglect the fields and hunting for their own people."

"What have you done to exert your authority?"

"If the villages want food, they work for it. Let them discipline their own young men." She walked to the kitchen. "We're going to need a welcoming feast in about a week's time. Start organizing now so our guests don't have to wait for days to be fed."

"What should we prepare?" The cook didn't stop stirring whatever was in the bowl.

"The Third Prince and his family are coming, probably with his staff and whoever else. Prepare something fit for the Prince. I don't know about his tastes, so cook what you like cooking."

"Yes, my lady."

Llathia left them to their work.

"The Third Prince's staal is not quite a day's walk from here, I'll need to send someone to make sure they haven't burnt it down since last time I was there."

"There is that much trouble there between Sombi and Congu?" Chiza pulled her to a stop.

"More between past overseer and slave. I told them to work it out without bloodshed, appointed some of the prince's staff to run the place. If they want to fight, they can go across the river. Honestly, I'll be happy to be done with the place."

"Sounds like being the Mtuaka is complicated."

"I try to make it run like an engine. All the parts need to be working properly and taken care of or it won't run or blows up. But I get push back at every turn. We should build up the warriors, or the priests, forget that the farmers feed us." She rolled her eyes and took a deep breath. "No one said it would be easy, but no one has challenged me in the past month."

"Challenged you?" Chiza scowled.

"Nobody who wasn't in Lusundi when I fought N'toox believes I killed him. They believe it now. I made them fight themselves, no champions since I had no champion. The heirs of those houses are much more polite now."

"You can't do everything yourself." Chiza shook her gently.

"I know, but if I don't, whoever I appoint makes it worse. The Mtuaka must have spent years hunting down anyone with the slightest competence."

"Doesn't surprise me." He hugged her. "The next challenger faces me." Chiza stood a head a half taller than Ilathia. His reputation was even greater than his size.

"I was hoping you'd say that. I get nightmares from those fights."

Chapter 3 The Wrong Foot

No matter what Cal tried to fix the relationship with kkitatin, it only made it worse. On the surface, the girl was disappointed in Cal's lack of heroism. But Cal remembered when she was a girl, when her father returned her mother got the biggest part of his attention. Her deportment classes always suffered when he returned and when he left again.

Being on the road to Roger's staal didn't make things easier. The jungle inland felt stifling, and the bugs were endemic. The road was more a well-marked path. Cal would have preferred to walk but needed to ride to keep up.

She was more than willing to cut kkitatin some slack, but the constant jibes wore on her. The language practice became torture sessions with Cal never sure if what she was learning was in fact Congu, or Sombi, or the equivalent of a sailor's cursing. She made sure to double-check the new words with Roger when she could. He kept extraordinarily busy on the way, meeting with complaining villagers, sending messengers back to Lusundi or ahead to his staal. He tried to spend time with kkitatin, but she was often asleep by the time his day ended.

"Roger, you need to take a special time with just you and kkitatin." Cal didn't want to spend her time talking about the girl. She was shocked at how quickly she got used to a second body in the bed and the ways to enjoy that body.

"Mmph." He sighed into the pillow.

"You made promises in blood to a living, breathing human being. To be a father, not someone in the distance."

He rolled over. "I have responsibilities, I spend most of those meetings with the villagers listening to how Lady Mtuaka is ignoring them, then backing up llathia. I report daily to father, and I'm getting reports from the staal, it has almost descended into chaos."

"One of your responsibilities is to kkitatin, or did your oath only mean when it was convenient?"

"Dammit, I'm doing my best." Roger sat up. "I've never done this before."

"Neither have I." Cal said, "but even I can see how unhappy she is."

"She has her own retainer."

"She doesn't want a retainer, she wants you."

"Fine." Roger rolled over ending the conversation.

Cal wanted to reach out, but a cold barrier between them stopped her. She hadn't felt anything like it since her father died.

Roger was up before Cal, he had kkitatin riding with him, talking animatedly pointing out things in the jungle to each other.

A woman named Luuca showed up to give language lessons. They were straightforward, and Cal didn't have to worry about what she was learning, but they weren't as interesting.

A day out from Lady Mtuaka's staal, a group of warriors with spears blocked the road. Roger unceremoniously put kkitatin down and pointed to the back of the line. She stomped back along the road, then into the jungle.

"That isn't good." Cal dismounted and followed the girl, hoping she was only a little way off the road. Kkitatin kept up a steady stream of complaint. It stopped abruptly with a squeak. Cal ran forward to see kkitatin backed up against a tree a huge black cat stared at her, tail twitching. Cal picked up a piece of wood and banged a tree. The cat stared at her but didn't back away. She stepped out in front of kkitatin and handed the girl the stick.

"Bang on the tree, make as much noise as you can."

"NO," Kkitatin shouted. "You may be First Wife, but I don't need you, I don't need anyone!"

The screaming was effective in making the cat decide to leave, but kkitatin immediately started walking again. Cal grabbed her arm.

"Stay here."

"I'm going back to the road." She tried to pull her arm away from Cal.

"Which way?" Cal spoke like a captain to a sailor who was doing something stupid. Kkitatin pointed in what looked like a random direction. "Are you sure?" Cal's voice was cold. "If you are wrong, we will only get more lost."

Kkitatin looked confused for a moment, then sneered at Cal.

"I am First Daughter; I will do what I want."

"I'm First Wife and I outrank you."

The princess dissolved into tears, wailing loud enough they could probably hear her on the road. A few minutes later one of Roger's warriors stepped out of the jungle and picked up kkitatin.

"Follow me."

It didn't take as long to get back to the road as it did to get lost, but it was in a completely different direction to where kkitatin pointed and very different from what Cal's best guess would have been.

"Kkitatin, ride in the wagon." Roger pointed, and kkitatin's face crumpled further.

"First Wife, you should know better. The warriors were looking for her immediately."

"There was a large black cat ready to make a meal out of your daughter and I didn't see a warrior around. That might have been a corpse your man carried back."

Roger looked like she'd slapped him.

"Ride on the wagon with kkitatin." He pointed, then spun and walked away. The people around her were very obviously not paying attention, so the fight would be the subject of gossip before they moved.

"Get out!" Kkitatin yelled at Cal.

"The Third Prince ordered me to ride with you." Cal settled herself. "And he ranks both of us."

***

For the next week, llathia didn't get to the cave once to check on the work. First Wife returned the day after she'd given her message. She smiled at Chiza, then retired to her rooms where she ran the web of informants who worked in the staal, and the region around it.

"Your guests will arrive tomorrow." First Wife informed llathia, "Mtuaka won't embarrass itself."

"Thanks, please inform the kitchen and other staff who will need to get ready."

In the morning, llathia took longer than usual to dress, asking Tashi several times what she should wear.

"You're the Lady Mtuaka," Tashi said. "As long as you have the colours on you, no one will worry about it. Everyone will be staring at the prince's first wife anyway."

The runner arrived at noon saying the prince and his entourage would be arriving within the hour. Llathia had to stop herself from running out immediately to wait.

"How do you do it?" Llathia ran her hands down Chiza's arm. "You are so calm."

"Focus like you are going into battle, then relax and wait for it to begin. As the prince's Right Arm, I had to be in the present to watch for dangers and traps."

Llathia went through the breathing and mental preparation she used before entering the arena. It felt like a surprisingly short time when the drums signalled her guests' arrival.

"Shall we?" Llathia walked out to the courtyard. The honour guard was in place, no one else carried a weapon larger than a knife. Chiza stood behind her and she drank in his calm.

"Welcome." Llathia smiled and saluted the prince, she had to force herself not to stare at the Anglian. She'd expected someone white like a lily, but the woman was more like baked bread. She looked around curiously, with bright blue eyes, but with a wide smile. Llathia's smile broadened as she noted how the woman brushed her hand against the prince. They had one thing in common.

"Lady Mtuaka," Prince Roger stepped forward to salute her. "You honour us with your welcome. Our hunters were fortunate, we have meat to offer for the feast."

"Thank you." Llathia hadn't expected that, but the kitchen would know what to do. "Take a moment to wash the dust from your faces." A young woman stepped forward with a pitcher of water, another with a towel.

Roger cupped his hands to receive water, splashed his face, then patted it dry with the towel. The Anglian woman stepped forward and washed her face without hesitation. Kkitatin moved more abruptly, as if she was in a bad mood.

"Come inside, I have some refreshments prepared, and some for your retainers as well.

"Lady Mtuaka," the prince presented the Anglian woman. "First Wife."

"Please call me Cal." Cal's voice was louder than Llathia expected.

"And of course you know, kkitatin, my First Daughter."

Kkitatin exchanged her glower for a brief smile. Llathia carefully restrained her sigh. It could be a troublesome visit.

***

"I'm sorry." Roger didn't look sorry, but Cal wasn't arguing. She didn't want to drive him from their room at Lady Mtuaka's staal.

"I am too."

"Kkitatin said there was no panther, but the warrior went back and found the prints. Why would she lie to me?"

"I'm the enemy, the one coming between her and the family she'd dreamed of the whole time you were away. Of course, she would do anything to drive a wedge between us."

"You're her mother."

"No, Roger, you're her father, I'm an interloper. I know why you're so busy. I was a ship's captain, I get it. That little girl doesn't, she was spoiled and neglected until you burst into her life and paid attention."

"But…" Roger stopped and closed his eyes. "I am supposed to bring Harasah together, and I can't even manage my own family."

"You don't need to manage your family; you need to love them. I told you from the start I wasn't doing a political marriage. I don't want to be First Wife to your Third Prince, I want to be Cal to your Roger. Kkitatin wants to be the special girl you made her feel like."

"I'm not sure I know how to do that."

"You'll figure it out." Cal caressed his cheek, then kissed him. "I will help the best I can, but at the moment, the best thing may be for me to stay busy out of the way. While you repair your relationship."

"She hates me now."

"No, she adores you, but she's hurt. Go apologize."

"Apologize to my daughter?"

"How else will she learn to say sorry?" Cal kissed him again. "Go talk to her, then come back so we can make up properly."

***

"Are you sure?" Roger held her hand.

"Yes, I will join you in a week or so. Make her feel like your princess."

He left. Cal watched him sweep kkitatin up with him on his horse, then they led the way toward his staal. Her arms were waving wildly as she talked.

"You must love her dearly," Lady Mtuaka came up beside her, "to let her separate you from your husband." The lady had the same fine bones as kkitatin and stood taller than Cal and muscular in a way that would have had the Anglian tongues flapping.

"I spent my childhood wishing for more time with my father. I understand what she feels." Cal took a deep breath. "Now, I haven't had a chance to see one of your engines yet, though I heard a lot about them."

"Very well, we can be there by noon. I'll find you some suitable clothes, mine will be too big."

The ride to the cave went quickly. Cal spent it trying to figure out what she was feeling, but it kept getting more tangled. She set it aside as they arrived at the village.

"This way." Lady Mtuaka waved a hand. They walked along a well-defined path. Then the jungle cleared away revealing a towering cliff with the cave looking tiny at the bottom. When they reached the cave, it stood as high as the Royal Engineers shed.

Eight people were clustered around a bulbous thing on a wagon. Smoke came from under it.

"That's a steam engine?" Cal jogged over to the wagon and walked around it. "I would never have thought about making one of wood. How do you keep it from burning? Ah, rock between the fire and the tank, but it would still be nerve-wracking to run. Wonder if I could make one with a barrel? Coal would burn hotter than wood, but that could be a problem too. Using belts to drive the wagon might work, but they'll probably slip."

"Sorry, but I don't understand Anglian." Lady Mtuaka stared at Cal with a bemused expression.

"I will try to translate into Congu."

Lady Mtuaka's expression didn't change as Cal stumbled through what she thought of the steam engine.

"…of course, iron is better, but I'm amazed at what you've accomplished."

"Engine Smith, who is this?" the largest of the men said.

"A guest." Lady Mtuaka said. "Be polite."

"Lady Mtuaka, I apologize for running on."

"Here I am Engine Smith."

"Engine Smith. I like that." Cal walked around the engine again. She spotted something that might have been a pressure release valve. Another valve gave them on/off power. A wild system of gears transferred power to a wheel with a belt, clearly intended to drive the wagon's axle. The axle was too narrow, not enough friction.

"If you have a larger wheel to transfer power from the engine to the wagon, the belt won't slip, and you should be able to get it moving." Cal spread her hands apart to show the size she thought would work best. It wouldn't be the most efficient system, but they could tweak it.

Soon the men and women had the wagon on blocks and taken off the wheel. Hovid, the big man, showed her the selection of gears they had. Cast iron, but standardized gears were a great idea. By the time the sun vanished from the sky, the wagon was chugging slowly across the clearing.

Chapter 4 A New Home

The village looked very different this time Roger approached it. No guards with guns watching over slaves in the fields. The fields looked ready for harvest but only a few desultory women picked produce.

"The houses have been repaired and the old slave barracks are dormitories for single adults. We have our own blacksmith and everything." Kkitatin pointed out the sights as they passed them. The headquarters had been completely refurbished to make his staal. It didn't look like an old army building. Carvings covered the wood pillars and beams. Furs hung on the walls and large windows caught the afternoon breeze.

"It all looks wonderful, my Queen." Roger dismounted, then helped kkitatin down.

Ttaoku met them at the door. "Welcome." He didn't look entirely happy to see them.

"I have heard there are issues between people," Roger said as he climbed the stairs. "Perhaps call them together so I may properly introduce myself."

"It isn't so easy to gather the people."

"Well, the ones who don't wish to come will miss the feast." Roger offered his hand. "My thanks for taking such good care of my man here." He waved at Voz'ci beside him. Ttaoku took his hand and his expression relaxed somewhat.

"I wonder how we could be so naïve as to think just telling the people to get along would make it happen. Once the princess left, things went back to being tense."

"It is why I'm here." Roger squeezed the chief's shoulder. "I would like to start by keeping you as chief. I will rule over the whole area ceded to me by the Mtuaka. If you have suggestions of people from either group who would be good advisors, pass their names to me."

That evening a crowd gathered divided into Sombi and Congu, they glared at each other.

"I won't have you wrecking my father's homecoming!" Kkitatin shouted from the stage in the village square. "You promised to be good." She put her hands on her hips. "If you can't smile, go home and you can go hungry."

"It isn't that easy, princess." Ttaoku leaned down to talk to her.

"You promised." She stomped her foot.

"You would really send us home hungry?" One of the Sombi came up and glowered at her.

"Would you feed your children if they lied to you?"

"It isn't that simple."

"Why not, ppaten?"

"Uh…"

"You aren't going to convince the princess that way." Ddokna jumped onto the stage. "Listen people, we gave an oath, all of us when we chose to live here. If it was easy, we wouldn't need an oath. We have one thing in common." He hoisted kkitatin to his shoulder. One of the Sombi started cheering, then some Congu joined in, soon it became a contest to see who could be louder.

Roger stepped forward and lifted his hands until the noise subsided.

"Friends, we are old and honourable enemies, now we work to becoming honourable friends. I propose that we stop calling ourselves Congu or Sombi."

"Then who are we?" ppaten asked.

"Who indeed? I suggest we call ourselves the Kkittu. We are bound by our common love for the princess. He pointed to her. "Let's enjoy this feast in her honour."

***

Early in the morning, Roger dressed in old clothes and headed out to the fields. A few women were there, and one gave him a basket and told him what spot to pick and what was ripe and what needed to stay. He worked until the sun heated the field to an uncomfortable level.

"Let's bring our harvest to the main square."

The women shrugged and they carried the baskets to the square.

"Third Prince, why are you working in the fields?" Ttaoku came over.

"If I don't, who will?" He put the basket on the stage. "I will be out in the fields tomorrow morning. It would be a sad thing if a soft prince like me could harvest more than all the men in the village."

He found kkitatin cleaning in the staal, a thunderous expression on her face.

"What happened to the staff from the village?"

34

"I fired them, they did nothing but argue about who should do what, so I'm helping the people you brought with you."

"What do you need me to do?"

Whenever there was argument about who should do what, Roger had his council go to mediate. If the people couldn't cooperate, they were sent to the fields or sent home with no food. After a week an angry crowd gathered in the square.

"Why are you starving us?"

"You treat us like slaves."

"What would you know about being slaves?"

"Silence!" Roger bellowed over the cacophony. "It is simple. When you were allowed to stay here, you took an oath to put the past behind you and treat each other with respect. You don't have to be best friends, but you will work together, or you will find another place to live. I don't think you will find a village that will allow you to live there and not work as hard as any other person. You have until tomorrow to decide. Now go home."

The people grumbled until ttaoku, ddokna and the rest of the council came up on the stage and stood behind Roger, arms crossed and unmoving.

"Where are we supposed to go?" A Congu woman demanded. "Our villages won't have us back, or they'll make us work like slaves."

"Are we supposed to swim across the river?" A Sombi man shouted. "And what will we do when we get there? Fight the Kershians?"

"That is your choice. To stay and do your share of the work, or leave and take your chances somewhere else."

"We'll take back our village and make it the way it was before." Men surged toward the stage. Shots echoed in the square and puffs of dust appeared in front of their feet.

"The next shot will not be a warning!" ttaoku shouted. "You were here before as soldiers under my command, by the kindness of the king you were allowed to bring your families. You shame yourselves by being in debt with your oathbreaking. Even the crocodiles won't eat such as you."

"I'm leaving." A Congu man picked up a bundle.

"That is your choice," Voz'ci said, "But once you pass that gate, you may not return. You will be under the rule of Lady Mtuaka. She has decreed that any who want to eat will work the harvest. It is your choice whether you harvest the Mtuaka's fields or your own."

"Where is the princess? She wouldn't do this to us."

"She is cleaning in the staal since none of you saw any honour in it. Shall I call her here and ask what she thinks of your oathbreaking?"

"You have until sunset to make your choice. If you choose to stay, you will renew your oath to the Third Prince and the princess. Break that oath and you will have no choice but to leave and take your chances wherever you go!" ttaoku shouted. "The council will remain to be sure there is no violence."

At sunset, a handful of men walked out the gate with nothing but the clothes on their back, none of the women would follow them.

The rest renewed their oath, pricking a finger and putting a spot of red on their foreheads.

"Tomorrow everyone goes to the field, there is food going to waste because of this foolishness," Roger said.

In the morning the fields were full of workers.

***

Astrid looked at the port of Pukhan, somewhere in that mass of people she had to find where Pentam Booksdale was, then get to him. Cal had suggested meeting with him first, before any other action. As soon as she began feeling out the other noble families of Kershia, she'd be painting a target on her back.

"Worrying again?" Gretta came to the rail and put her hand on Astrid's. "We start at the Anglian Embassy ship and go from there."

"It will be watched."

"I expect so, we'll need to go in disguise, maybe have an adult accompany us."

"I can ask Paul; he'd likely pay a courtesy call anyway. Let's go find the Purser and see if we can get an appointment.

The morning after the ship made landing, the first mate of the Griffin sauntered along the dock to the Anglian embassy ship accompanied by a young couple holding hands. They walked up the gangplank and a few minutes later were sitting with Captain Jenkins Hashmick.

"Heard about Shillingsworth, shame, she was a true firecracker."

"We're friends of hers." Astrid sat straight and took her cap off. "She suggested we find Pentam Booksdale and ask for help."

"Pentam Booksdale, huh, just like that?" The captain waved at the side table. "You mind pouring tea? This is going to take a while."

Astrid held up a hand at Gretta's horrified face. "Would you like milk, captain?"

"No, clear is fine." Astrid handed him a cup, but Paul waved off her offer. She brought cups for her and Gretta, then resettled herself.

"First off, introductions." Captain Hashmick pointed at Astrid. "How do you know Admiral Shillingsworth?"

"We met her on the Griffin, sir. Commander McAllen suggested that Cal stay dead for the time being, but she is very much alive." Astrid sipped at her tea and raised her eyebrows.

"Say she is alive, why should I believe you. Next, you will be claiming to be the lost heir to Kershia."

"At your service." Astrid swivelled the seal on her finger and lifted it up for the captain to see. He froze in place long enough for Gretta to start giggling.

"I got McAllen's dispatch just yesterday. Why didn't you say something, lass, I mean, Your Highness?"

"It's more fun this way." Astrid shrugged. "Very good tea by the way." She took a long sip.

"I suppose, but it is hard on an old man's heart. What can I, unofficially, do for the Imperial Princess?"

"My name is Astrid, I would be more comfortable if you used that, I already have an assassin on my tail, courtesy of my uncle. I would like to keep knowledge of my identity quiet until the time is right."

"Of course," the captain put his cup to one side. "I can send a message to the Ambassador in Hanginj."

"I didn't think we had embassies inside Zithaya."

"When Anglia released the details of the Michoro Engine to the world, Her Majesty received an invitation to send an ambassador to the capital. It was through him that Mr. Booksdale was asked to travel to Zithaya to talk about his work."

"I see." Astrid thought while staring into her cup. "How useful would it be to Anglia to have a friendly person sitting on the Imperial throne?"

"Civil war is an ugly thing, lass."

"I don't intend on fighting a war." Astrid lifted her hand. "There is a law in place which allows a member of the royal family to call the Emperor to account. It has happened twice in our history, the first time the member of the royal family died suddenly before they could officially present their case. In the second instance, the Emperor was stripped of his ruling power and the throne went to the next in line. I would say I have fifty-fifty odds. I'm fourth in line for the throne, but holding the seal will mean acknowledging me a part of the royal family."

"Anglia can't interfere in Kershia's internal affairs."

"I'm not asking for interference, captain, just an introduction to Mr. Booksdale."

Someone knocked at the door.

"Come."

"Sir, the watch wishes to report a change in surveillance. The Kershians have increased their number."

"Do they think they can take the ship?" Captain Hashmick shook his head. "Triple the watch, all hands to be ready for hostile action."

"Aye, sir." The sailor left and closed the door.

"I'm their target." Astrid clasped her hands to keep them from shaking. "I would rather not be the cause of more death."

"We can hardly walk you out past the watchers, they'll be on you in an instant. Outside the wall, Zithaya doesn't worry so much about what happens."

"If I stay here, Sigrid will make her move. I expect she has complete plans of the ship."

"Let's say I was going to infiltrate the ship with a small force. I'd create a distraction and climb up the rear. We're working on a repair that affects the security of the ship."

"How does that help us?" Gretta asked.

"What do you call an ambush you know about?" The captain grinned wickedly. "A trap."

***

Late in the evening two days after they'd boarded the embassy ship a fight broke out on the dock by the gangway. Security details jogged to positions where they could control access to the ship by the stairs or ropes.

Sigrid climbed the side of the ship away from the action, followed by three others all in dark clothing. No one spotted them. With hand signs, she directed them to follow the orders they'd been given. She then crept along the gangways. Gunfire sounded, echoing through the deserted corridor. That would pull more Anglians from their positions. The fight would escalate to shooting at the ship. The Zithayan isolationists would get the blame for the night's action. A second burst of gunfire came from a different direction.

Sigrid opened the door slowly to the room she had chosen to begin her search. No response. She slipped in and swept the room with her gun. Nothing. Too much to expect it to be that easy. Sigrid searched the room and came up with a ring of keys. She frowned at them. Nothing to do but take the bait.

The third man must have been caught as no more gunfire came from inside the ship. She loped along the gangway and down into the ship. The brig was not only positioned to keep people in, but also to keep people out. The Marines guarding the door fidgeted slightly.

She expected they were closing in behind her. Sigrid gave up on stealth and dashed back up along a different path. Someone moved to her left and she fired. Shots returned from her right, they pinged into the walls as she ran past. She almost missed her turn, skidding to get around the corner, then shooting out the lock of the room she wanted.

Bullets buzzed past her, one hitting her arm. She slammed the door behind her and ran to the hatch where she spun the wheel to open it. The door behind her burst open as she pulled the hatch in. She fell bonelessly out into the harbour as a hail of bullets hit the hatch and the walls around her.

Nothing vital hit, Sigrid swam down until a swimmer met her and guided her to an opening in the underwater boat.

She hated getting shot, but she had the information she wanted. The princess was in Zithaya and probably heading for the capital.

"Head out to the rendezvous with the gunboat and get me some bandages."

Chapter 5 Claiming the Hunt

Llathia glared at Cal, but the Anglian woman was oblivious. The crew gathered around her as she waved her hands. Things were moving faster than they ever had. In other circumstances, llathia would have been delighted. Or so she told herself.

She had nothing to do in her own shop. Cal was unfailingly polite and always asked permission for each project she started. But each time it closed a door on something llathia wanted to try. She should be thankful for more time to fulfill her duties as the Mtuak, but she wanted to be the engine smith. She wanted the rush when something worked, even the despair when it all failed.

"How long are you going to let this go on?" First Wife appeared behind her with the uncanny timing she had.

"What do you mean?"

"You know exactly what I mean." First Wife narrowed her eyes in the slightest of frowns.

"She means well."

First Wife snorted. "What she means has nothing to do with it. Either take back your hunt or leave it. Mooning from the edge of the crowd is beneath you. You fought to be the Mtuaka, now you need to fight to be the engine smith."

"I don't know that challenging her in the arena will help. The Third Prince would be upset if I killed his wife."

"There is more than one way to fight." First Wife waved away the topic. "There are some warriors who need your attention."

"The ones the Third Prince tossed from his staal. Why can't they just realize that everyone works?" Llathia sighed. "I might as well deal with them."

"It will give you a chance to vent your spleen, then you'll think straight."

Llathia led the way back to the village, then took a horse to ride to the staal.

"Bring me the bandits." Llathia dropped into her chair. Soon two hands of men stood glowering at her.

"You left the Third Prince's staal, now you've been causing trouble in my lands. Prince Roger warned you. My patience has run out. You are banished from Mtuaka. My warriors will take you across the river and you can try living in Sombi. I will allow you to keep the clothes you are wearing."

"We earned our gear." The biggest of the men yelled at her.

"You stole and extorted everything you own from my people. It will remain here."

The big man charged forward, before her guards could react, llathia rammed her spear through the man's heart. She wrenched it out and waved the bloody weapon in from of the nine remaining bandits.

"Any other argument?" The men stepped back and three of them dropped to their knees.

"The standing ones can swim to Sombi, the rest, take in a boat drop them and return. If they fight, knock them senseless, but they will be off my land by sundown."

Her guards saluted and the warriors escorting the prisoners pushed them out of the hall.

"Feel better?" First Wife asked as she brought over wine for llathia.

"Sit, drink with me." Llathia took a cup and sipped at it. "By rights, I should have executed the lot of them."

"I doubt many of them will survive the river. The crocodiles are indiscriminate in what they eat."

"I want to give them a chance."

"Really? If you insist." First Wife played with her cup. "When you hunt, who determines what prey you will take?"

"I do of course."

"What about the other hunters?"

"They do what I tell them if they ever want to hunt with me again." Llathia slouched back into her chair. "I get it." She looked at the pieces of the problem. Cal wasn't the issue, or at least not directly. "I need to get back to work."

***

Something undefinable had changed in the Mtuaka. She reminded Cal of some of the admirals when they woke up and took control.

"Cal, I want you to refurbish what you can of the iron engine in the boat at the dock. Take Hovid with you. Make sure he learns what he needs to."

"Yes, Lady Mtuaka." Cal nodded at her, then headed toward the village. "Get a move on, Hovid."

They spent the night at the Mtuaka staal, then headed for the Kkittu village. There were people working harvesting in the fields. A warrior at the gate waved them in and detailed a young girl to guide them to the staal.

"Oh, it's you." Kkitatin rolled her eyes. "Father is around somewhere." She walked back into the staal. "Don't stand there watching," Kkitatin said. "You've got the rest of this floor to clean."

"But we cleaned…" the woman sighed and picked up a cloth. "Yes, princess."

"Hovid, go find that boat Lady Mtuaka was talking about."

He shrugged and ambled off.

Cal wandered through the staal asking people, until finally someone knew where Roger was working and led them to him.

"Welcome back." He looked up from the books he was working in and stretched. "Thank you for giving us some time. I think it helped a lot."

"Glad to hear it. She wasn't thrilled to see me, but she didn't set the dogs on me."

Roger laughed.

"Do you want a tour?"

"Sure."

Roger took her hand and showed her around the building. It didn't have the confusing hallways of the kraal in Lusundi, but rooms opened into other rooms seemingly at random and staircases appeared in odd places.

"Here are the rooms kkitatin chose for me. Hers are across the hall."

"Did she try to put me in the stables?"

"At the end of the hall." Roger laughed. "It is Congu tradition for the men and women to have separate quarters, but there are rooms beside me that are empty. More importantly, we set aside a workspace on the ground level for you. They indeed used to be a stable."

"My first workshop was a carriage house, as long as I have a place to make a mess, I'm happy. Lady Mtuaka asked me to refurbish the engine from some old boat."

"That's more or less floating by the dock. We'll need to have someone standing by in case the crocs get hungry."

Hovid waited for her at the front door.

"Wouldn't call what's there a boat, but it's this way." He led the way as if Roger didn't know his own village.

The boat sat mostly underwater, leaning against the wooden pier.

"Nobody knew how to maintain it, so they left it to fill up and sink during the rainy season."

"You have to love a challenge."

***

"Pull the rope tight, but don't try to haul it yet." Cal sloshed around in the boat checking the air bladders she'd fastened to the side, then pumped more air in until the boat shifted.

"Now."

Hovid walked around the capstan carefully stepping over the rope each time around.

"Hold it there!" Cal yelled. "We'll need more lines on it, but it will work."

It took another week, but they dragged it up on the shore. Then Cal started the process of dismantling the engine and boiler and transferring it to the workshop.

She and Hovid, along with a crowd of young helpers, scrubbed the rust off the engine parts.

"I'm going to concentrate on the boiler and the engine. You pull out all the gears and other parts, organize them over to the side on the bench."

They toiled away, the boiler had some surface rust, but nothing that looked like it would cause a rupture. The entire machine was taken apart, checked, and reassembled. Cal paid particular attention to the valves and gauges.

"Time for a pressure test." Cal ordered everyone out of the shop and fired up the boiler. She just planned enough pressure to check the seals and valves. Everything checked out. She let the fire go out and sighed. "That's it for now. We build a safety wall before we run the engine."

The wall took another day, so Cal checked over everything the tenth or twentieth time.

The Lady Mtuaka showed up for the engine test.

"I've never been this close to an iron engine before." She inspected it carefully, especially the pressure gauge. "This would make things much easier."

"We can order some from Anglia." Cal looked over at her.

"I could." Lady Mtuaka smiled. "Let's talk about what we can order from your people, after the test."

The steam engine ran perfectly, and Lady Mtuaka's grin grew wider.

"Could this power an airship?"

"A small one." Cal looked at the engine and ran the numbers in her head. "A one- or two-person possibly. It would be better as an auxiliary engine maybe running steam cannons."

"We will talk more about that, but we need a ship before we can arm it."

"You're right about that."

"I will build the ship; you arm it."

"Are you sure? I've already built airships."

"You think because I'm Congu, I can't build a ship, only you Anglians are smart enough?"

The words slashed at Cal, she hadn't noticed the anger in the engine smith, but like kkitatin's, it boiled just below the surface as dangerous as any boiler. The choice was to argue and probably alienate the woman completely or trust she could do what she said.

"I didn't invent the airship," Cal said. "Some guy in Ferandica made it work, I just took it and improved it. I have no doubt you can do what you say. I will create what you need to make it a war ship."

Chapter 6 Running Dark

Emperor Heodvolt paced in the small office. His stomach burned with acid.

"Why haven't we taken Sombi back? It's been months."

"A rushed campaign could be disastrous." General Mizvrat leaned back in his chair, not bothering to follow the emperor with his eyes. "We go in when we're ready, the airships will be built soon, and we have enough warships to support them. Let them prepare as much as they want, no Harasahn country can match the empire."

"The people want to see action."

"The people are fickle. Make a mistake and they'll turn on you. You're the Emperor. You don't need to worry about the people. Stop borrowing money from the war mongers. They don't care who wins as long as they get to sell their goods."

"What about the girl?"

"My agent says she's in Zithaya, we have operatives with the isolationist groups. She won't last long."

"They didn't kill that Booksdale person."

"He's crippled. That's the next best thing to being dead."

***

Pentam drove his chair into the room. He was curious about these girls who had convinced the Zithayans to let them visit him. They couldn't be anyone he knew, maybe they were interested in the Michoro engine.

"Mr. Booksdale." The taller girl stood and bowed. "So glad you could see us. I am Astrid, and my companion is Gretta." She waved at the darker-haired girl, who stood and curtsied. "I believe you already know Bundo."

Pentam glanced over at the scarred, dark-skinned man. "It is good to see you Bundo. I wondered what you were doing after Cal…" He trailed off and had to wipe his eyes.

"Cal asked us to come and see you." Astrid handed him a kerchief. "I would appreciate if you didn't spread the word that she is alive. It isn't time for her return from the dead."

"Cal's alive?" Pentam lowered his voice from a shout. "How do I know you aren't playing some kind of game?" The sudden suspicion made his heart ache.

"An understandable concern, she doesn't have any proof of life. That is part of the reason for me asking you not to spread the word. Do you remember the day you had a conversation with Cal outside the hotel in Finches Harbour? You were worried because you'd fallen in love with Crysabel. Cal told you she was too busy with the engines. You said, 'I'm being dumped for an engine?'"

"It's true." Pentam laughed, then dabbed as his eyes again. "But you didn't come all the way to Hanginj to tell me that."

"Not just to tell you that, no." Astrid sighed. "How familiar are you with the situation with the Kershian Empire?"

"You mean aside from them wanting to rule the world?"

"They can't win a head-to-head war with Anglia and it would probably bankrupt both countries, so they've turned their attention to Harasah. They have already installed a puppet king in the desert kingdom and failed an attempt to do so in Sombi. I fully expect they are preparing to attack Sombi with an overwhelming force. By the time Anglia hears, it will be too late. Harasah will give Kershia unlimited resources."

"You are well versed for a young girl so far from home."

"It is my duty to be aware of what is happening in the world."

"So you came to me to get to the Zithayans? What makes you think they will meet with you, even if you are a friend of Cal's?"

"They won't meet with young Astrid, but they may want to talk to a member of the Kershian royal family and an heir to the throne."

"And I am to believe you?"

"She is what she claims." Bundo spoke from his post near the door. "The killers they've sent after her are proof enough."

"I will ask the Secretary, but I can make no promises."

"That is all I can ask." Astrid leaned forward and suddenly looked younger. "You want to hear what Cal was doing before I met her?"

***

Commander Kelly Landers took a deep breath. The ship was claustrophobic at best, but it ran beneath the ocean and didn't leak. That in itself was a major step forward.

"You make anything from the pings?"

"It's tricky, but I at least have the big picture. Two objects on the surface, I can't see the bottom. Turn sixty degrees port, I want to check something."

When they returned to their slip, Kelly was sweating but pleased with the test. The bigger ship would be ready in a month. Then it would need to take its shakedown cruise.

"We go out again tomorrow. We need to learn how to navigate with just the pings."

"Yes, commander."

The Kershians had a ship out there ramming other ships, or that's what she'd heard. They couldn't be allowed the ability to attack with impunity. Wherever humans could go, Anglia had to reign supreme.

***

Cal wanted a break from destruction. She preferred to create for scientific purposes. The world didn't agree with her. Yet today she was testing destruction.

In the stable, the Improbable Two was taking shape. Cal told herself at some point she'd have to air test the weapon designs, but she didn't think Lady Mtuaka would be happy. Two was even simpler than her first little airship. Really, she should call it a hot air balloon with a propeller.

"Cal, the test setup is ready," Hovid reported with his usual lack of enthusiasm. Lady Mtuaka had left him to be her assistant, and probably to report on her progress. That was fine. He didn't know about Two, at least she didn't think he did. When she tested the ship would be when the cat was out of the bag.

The setup for the test was simple. They aimed at a balloon which moved fitfully in the breeze in front of a tall wooden fence.

Rainy weather had socked in but waiting for good weather for a test was a fool's game.

At least the silky, air-proof fabric didn't absorb much water.

"All clear, everyone accounted for and behind the line," Hovid told her. "It seems like a lot of fuss for a little disc."

"Safety comes first. Lady Mtuaka would be annoyed if I got you or anyone else killed."

"I heard you were testing the thing." Kkitatin huddled under a cloak.

"As long as you do what I say, you can watch."

"Hmmmph," Kkitatin grumbled but stayed behind the line with Roger and a few other onlookers.

"First test of the thing." Cal double-checked the setup. It was a side-armed trebuchet that flung discs at high speed. They'd tested the ammunition by hand, and it flew reasonably straight. Perfect wasn't an issue with the size of the expected target. "Everything in readiness. Ready to fire, in three, two, one."

The arm snapped forward and the disc flew out, then soared high into the air before tumbling into the river.

"The disk didn't come off the arm level." Cal poked around with the launcher and adjusted where the grip held the disc.

"Ready to arm?" Hovid asked.

"Arm."

He cranked back the arm until it trembled with the stored energy. Cal clicked the lock in place, then loaded the next disc.

"Ready to fire in three, two, one."

This time the disc ploughed into the ground sending mud as far as the balloon.

It took five more shots before the disc flew level and straight to slash through the balloon and hit the fence behind. They found the disc embedded in the wood fence, deep enough even Hovid couldn't free it.

On the sixth shot, the arm snapped, flinging wood in a wide arc between the watchers and the balloon.

"It broke," Hovid said. "I guess we didn't build it right."

"Five shots at full power, now we need to dial in the balance between what is effective and what destroys the weapon. Well done." Cal examined the broken arm. "We're done for today, shows over."

She put out the fire under the balloon and checked how it stood up to the weather. The seams were tight, the glue was easier and faster than sewing, but she'd feared it would come apart in the damp.

"Impressive." Roger inspected the fence and the hole in the balloon.

"I'd like to make a bigger hole, bring the enemy down faster, but a bigger disc will lessen the force of the hit."

"I'm sure you'll work it out." Roger brushed his hand on her shoulder, about as close as he got to public affection. "You're like a different person when you are engineering." He used the Anglian word and she had to fit the meaning into Congu. Cal was thinking in Congu now and wondered if she'd be able to speak in Anglian or Kershian again easily. How Roger kept all the languages he knew separate, she didn't know.

***

Llathia sat in the dark in her room at the staal and tried to imagine how to make an elephant fly. For all their huge wings, eagles were surprisingly light. She couldn't make wings big enough for what she needed, but maybe a person? She started to come up with ways to make huge wings, rigid like a soaring eagle. Maybe she'd better start small, like Cal. She didn't know if the Anglian woman was infuriating in spite of or because of her competence.

The rafters supporting the roof were triangles, if she made something out of twigs, then covered it with fabric? She went out in the hall. A warrior straightened as she left her room.

"How may I serve?"

"I'm looking for twigs, half the thickness of my smallest finger, as long as my forearm."

"There are reeds by the child river, would they work?"

"Only one way to find out."

He insisted on accompanying her into the damp weather. "Could be crocs."

She carried her own spear and he carried two.

The river was high because of the wet weather after checking for predators, the warrior let her wade into the mud to pick out suitable reeds.

I wonder what he is thinking, his Lady clambering in the mud. She had her arms full of reeds when a log near her opened its eyes and lunged toward her. Llathia dropped the reeds and snatched her spear from its sling on her back. She fell backward aiming her spear into the gaping maw of the beast. She thought it was going to come the whole length of the spear. It jammed with only an arm's length between them. The crocodile roared and chomped at the spear until the warrior put one of his through the creature's eye into its brain.

"Are you uninjured, my Lady?"

"Only bruised." Llathia struggled to her feet and picked up her reeds to carry them to firm ground.

"Once you are safe, I will return for the crocodile."

"Bring help, there may be more."

"As you say, my Lady." He took the reeds from her and tucked them under an arm. "What made you think to drop low and use the spear like a boar spear?"

"My feet were stuck in the mud. I didn't have much choice."

"I've heard stories, but I never thought to be privileged to see my Lady hunt."

"Hardly a hunt," Llathia said. "Falling on my butt."

"The crocodile is dead, and you are alive. That is a successful hunt."

"We could use a feast." Llathia rubbed her side where the butt of the spear had bruised her.

***

The feast was a great way to break up the dullness of the rainy season. Adults talked and got caught up, children played with friends or made new friends.

Llathia relaxed beside Chiza and watched her people enjoy themselves. She allowed herself a cup of wine. As she went to take a sip something landed in her drink, splashing her face.

A young boy prostrated himself in front of her. "Sorry, sorry." Almost in tears.

"What is this?" She plucked the thing out of the wine. It had a stem and two 'leaves.'

"You spin it, and it goes into the air." The boy jumped up. "Let me show you."

She gave him the thing. He spun the stem between his hands and the toy lifted off almost to the rafters. Llathia caught it as it descended.

"Get your friends and bring them here."

"Yes, my Lady." The boy bolted into the crowd shouting. A few minutes later a crowd of children and youth gathered in front of her.

"Please, don't be hard on them." A girl stepped forward, perhaps twelve or thirteen. "I should have told them to be more careful."

"You made this?"

"Yes, my Lady." The girl gulped but didn't look away.

"Fascinating. Where did the idea come from?" She spun it like the boy had shown her and it floated up on an angle, soaring across the hall to land in front of an old woman. She picked it up, then spun to send it back to the children, chuckling the whole time. Llathia waved to her, and the old woman nodded back.

"There are seeds which spin, building our own means they last longer, and go farther.

"We are going to have a contest, with teeth from my crocodile as prizes. One for the highest height reached, the other for the longest distance travelled. You can build it as large as you like. We hold the contest in seven days."

Llathia handed the toy back to the girl who stared mouth open at Lady Mtuaka.

"Off you go now. Have fun." The children roared out of the hall babbling with excitement.

Chapter 7 Prototype

Cal climbed into her seat on Two and pedalled. She'd cobbled together extra gears and pieces into a frame that held the propeller. The blades spun, not quite humming. Good, though she'd need to exercise more if she planned on a long flight. She leaned back and puffed taking in the wood stables, now cleared out to make one large workspace. A fire in here would be a disaster. She'd just have to be extra careful.

The next step would be to inflate the balloon and do a tethered test. Cal looked forward to getting back into the sky.

"So the project is coming along well?" Roger leaned in the doorway.

"More or less." Cal wiped her face on a towel. "Next is a tethered test for buoyancy, then I go up and try the propeller."

"Sounds dangerous." Roger frowned.

"That's why I break it into baby steps. That way a failure doesn't kill me."

"I'm happy you have staying alive as a priority." He walked over and spun the propeller with a finger. "Ouch, sharp."

"Sorry, should have warned you, I used steel from the boat's heat shield for the prop, but it isn't well finished."

"No matter." Roger sucked on his finger. "I need to go away, maybe for a month. Our neighbours are unsure of the alliance. Look after kkitatin while I'm away, maybe she'll warm up to you if I'm not around to make her jealous."

"We can only hope." Cal sighed. "I failed to live up to her expectations, now nothing I do is good enough."

"She's young, she'll come around."

"Young and stubborn." Cal laughed. "But I'm pretty stubborn myself. Go, do what you need to do. I'll keep things on an even keel here."

***

The next day only drizzled, so Cal had Hovid and a couple of other warriors help pull the Two out of the stable into the open space they had tested the disc thrower. The river flowed sluggishly past, mist hiding the far bank.

"Lady Mtuaka said she'd build the airship." Hovid frowned.

"And she will, but she didn't forbid me from building one for my own use."

"She'll be angry." The frown grew deeper.

"Very likely." Cal double-checked the rope tethering the Two to the ground and the lighter one running up to the release to drop the lid on the brazier to bring her back to earth as a crowd of curious onlookers gathered.

"Load the sandbags on the platform. We'll pull them off one by one until she goes up. If the rope breaks, let it go."

"Another weapon test?" kkitatin put her hands on her hips, but Cal didn't have time to stop and explain everything

"Not exactly." Cal arranged the balloon to catch the hot air from the brazier, but not catch on fire itself. "Watch carefully from a safe distance. Remember how the disc thrower failed."

Kkitatin moved back.

The balloon filled up slowly, then grew taught and the platform shifted.

"Stand back!" Cal shouted as the Two lifted ungainly into the sky. A sandbag fell and the platform rocked. "Get away from the ropes, and stay out from underneath, looks like we might lose her."

The rocking diminished and the Two reached the end of the rope, it creaked but held.

"Wow!" kkitatin shouted. "It's flying."

Cal pulled the lighter rope and the lid fell onto the brazier, smothering the fire. An hour later the Two settled gently on the ground.

"I'd say that is a success." Cal had the men put the Two away after the fire was well and truly doused.

***

Three days later they pulled the Two out again, this time Cal climbed aboard and belted herself into the seat as the fire filled the balloon.

"I want to come." Kkitatin crossed her arms and pouted.

"Not this one, princess." Cal touched a sandbag with her toe and nudged one. Good, she could reach; she'd added a system to bleed off hot air without completely deflating the balloon. Between that and the sandbags, she had control of vertical movement. The prop could be swivelled about thirty degrees in either direction to make for a cumbersome steering mechanism.

The Two lifted off, Cal left the tether rope attached at both ends. It lifted faster than the Improbable, Cal eased some of the air out of the envelope to ease the sudden stop at the end of the rope. Even so, without her being belted in, she'd have fallen. The rope attached at the nose, Cal pedalled hard trying to get slack in the rope, but she just went higher.

A noise grabbed her attention. Cal swivelled until she faced the noise. Gunfire, lots of it. A cloud of steam travelled from where Roger'd said the village on the other shore stood. It could only mean a train had arrived. She let the heat out of the balloon as fast as she dared. The landing shook her badly and she couldn't get the belt undone. As the balloon dropped on the brazier it caught fire.

Cal stopped, took a deep breath and pulled the tiny, but wickedly sharp blade out of the stick she used to keep her hair up, now that it had grown out. A quick slice and she was free and rolling across the ground. Cold water sluiced over her. Kkitatin stared down at her.

"You okay?"

"I think so." Cal groaned and sat up. The Two was engulfed in flame. "Make sure the fire doesn't spread, otherwise let it burn out. There's trouble on the other side of the river. I heard a lot of gunfire and saw what had to be a steam engine." The Kershians must have made a push and got up this far. They have a clear track up to the coal mine. "I need to talk to Lady Mtuaka." She gently touched a bruise on her forehead. It would keep.

Chapter 8 Kershian Resurgence

"The Kershians have been pushing hard. They'd built a fort around the tree that we felled on the tracks, first my people knew of the cleared track was a train full of soldiers with the latest guns. The desert kingdom is supplying them. Now they have the north end of the track to the coal mine and south to the farming district." Ttaoku walked beside Cal and kkitatin. "Prince Roger was hoping to have the alliance in place before something like this happened. The Sombi have pulled back into the deep jungle." Cal sweated in the warm rain.

"I didn't know it was balanced on such a knife-edge." Cal frowned. "We need to move things faster."

"Lady Mtuaka will send a message to the king, but any action aside from that is up to her."

"The Kershians will bring up boats like the one you took apart and invade kkittu" kkitatin frowned.

The Mtuaka staal came into sight. A crowd had gathered in front of the staal. Lady Mtuaka looked up and scowled. She said something to a young girl standing next to her, then stalked over to them.

"You three didn't come together with good news."

"The Kershians have taken yyatha on the other side of the river. The Sombi have been forced into the jungle. We fear their next target may be kkittu. We don't know how many boats with iron engines they have." Ttaoku said. "But they timed the push for when the river was in flood."

"Why now?" Lady Mtuaka peered suspiciously at them. "My own sources told me about the Keishians being more active, but nothing about losing the village."

"They used the train to break through the blockade. If they keep moving it will be hard to drop another tree on the tracks." Cal breathed deeply. "I saw the smoke from the train."

"From across the river, you saw this?" Lady Mtuaka fixed her with a glare.

"From my flying machine."

"We agreed you were building weapons. I was to build the airship."

"I built it for my personal use, it would be useless as a warship."

"You lied to me."

"I didn't agree not to build something for myself. It is Roger's staal."

"Words." Lady Mtuaka shouted. "You couldn't stop yourself from showing off. I will pass the word to watch the river, but Roger's staal can deal with any Kershians on their own."

"I'm sure you will be able to build the airship, but the time to do so is short. Will you let pride keep you from the resources you need to defend your country? If Sombi falls, Congu won't be far behind."

"Not while I breathe." Lady Mtuaka spoke icy cold. "Now you must leave, I will not have you on my land."

"I did what I had to." Cal met the lady's gaze with one just as cold. "I hope you live up to your own expectations. I will send

Hovid to you. He knows how to build the weapons to arm your ship." She spun on her heel and headed back on the long walk to kkittu. Kkitatin caught up with Cal.

"You've made a bad enemy."

"It's too bad, but the Kershians aren't going to wait around while we chat politely."

"What do you plan to do?"

"We'll start by fortifying kkittu and keeping our people safe."

The goods she'd ordered arrived and miraculously the boiler accompanied the piles of fabric and the metal tubes and gears. She put everything in the stable and concentrated on what they needed to defend the village.

***

"The Anglian woman is infuriating, but she's unfortunately right. We don't have time to play." Llathia paced in her room while Chiza leaned against the wall. "I am moving to the cave. I have the winning whirligigs; they'll give me a start."

"Who is going to run the staal?"

"First Wife can keep it running on the day by day, if something else comes up, we're only a half-day away."

"Before you go, consider sending messages across the river. Our warriors who want to fight so badly may as well defend their own villages. We have a lot of people in Lusundi, maybe call them back, we need to inform the king in any case."

"You're right." Llathia let go of her rage, stomped it down and banked it like the fire under the boiler. "I will send the messages tomorrow before we leave."

***

Llathia played with the winning whirligig trying to decide how best to use it. Her reed eagle glided like a rock. She was missing something about the wings. What kept the eagle soaring without moving a feather?

"Hovid." She shouted.

"Yes, Engine Smith." He approached warily.

"I need to watch eagles, you know this area, where's a good place?"

"Up on the cliff. There's a back way up, but it takes two days."

"Find someone to guide me. You need to work on the weapons and the airship." Llathia had swallowed her pride and soaked up everything Hovid knew about making the envelope and what the flying machine looked like.

The hike to the top of the cliff wasn't just two days, it was a brutal two days, only Chiza's support kept her moving, but they arrived to a stunning view. She couldn't see any evidence of the workshop below, even the village was hidden in the trees. The jungle stretched out like the ocean before her.

Eagles soared beneath them, coming close enough for llathia to see the curve of their wings. She played with twigs, cloth and the glue the Anglian used for the fabric balloon. The little birds plunged off the cliff, but slowly over two days of experimenting they started gliding farther.

"Okay, time to get back down." Llathia looked wistfully at the cliff. If only she had wings. She barely noticed the hike, letting Chiza guide her while she imagined how to make wings big enough for a person to glide like an eagle. The curve on the top was more important than the shape, if she used triangles for strength, maybe she could keep it lightweight.

"What's the strongest and lightest wood we can get?"

"There are giant reeds in a forest on the other side of this mountain." The guide, Fahtin said.

"How hard would it be to get some?"

"I know some people who could be convinced." Fahtin shrugged. "The hard part will be getting them down the mountain."

"Don't worry about that." Llathia smiled. "I have an idea for that."

When they arrived in camp, Hovid had a balloon floating above the clearing.

"It is still too small to lift a person." He frowned. "We're waiting on more fabric from Lusundi, should be here tomorrow or the day after.

"Would it float to the top of the cliff?"

"Probably."

"Fahtin, you and your friends go harvest the reeds. Long as you can get, but no thicker than your wrist. Pile them at the top of the cliff.

Llathia took the next week to make a balloon large enough and safe enough to do what she wanted. She decided to make a basket instead of a platform, it only needed to go up and down.

"You aren't getting in that basket." Chiza stood arms crossed. "A warrior has volunteered. We only have one engine smith."

"I guess you're right, I was looking forward to flying."

"You will get your chance."

The warrior climbed in with a stoic face, but her knuckles were pale on the side of the basket.

"Keep the fire going, but not big enough to light the balloon." Hovid handed her the bow and the arrows with the roped already tied to them.

"You will be the first Congu to soar." Llathia put a hand on the basket. "I'm envious."

The basket took off trailing a long rope. Not enough to reach the top of the cliff, but Anda had been told it would be enough to reach the ground when the balloon got to the peak.

They watched the balloon ascend then successfully be caught by the warriors on the edge. Soon after the balloon began to descend.

"Everyone get in the cave," Llathia ordered her crew. "If the ropes come loose, you don't want to be underneath."

The journey down came without incident until the balloon started dropping faster. Llathia watched from a safe distance, fists clenched. The bundle of giant reeds crashed into the ground, the basket hit and tipped over, scattering glowing embers about.

"Grab the balloon, keep it from the coals!" Llathia shouted as she ran, then tried to hold the fabric over her head until other hands lifted and carried it away from danger.

Anda climbed out, holding her arm.

"I think it's broken. I should have kept the fire up more and taken more time to descend. It's my fault."

"Don't worry about that now." Llathia wrapped an arm around the warrior and helped her out of the way of the bustle of people rescuing the balloon and basket while making sure no fires started.

Chapter 9 Invasion

Cal wanted to start on another air ship immediately, but defending the village took priority. They built a bank of the disc throwers hoping they'd be as effective against a boat as they were the fence behind the test envelope.

Cal used Roger's name to order some material from the Lusundi smiths but wasn't going to wait to find out if or when the stuff would arrive.

"We put the crank and loading behind a wall to protect the warriors. If we run out of discs, use anything that will stay on the spring arm."

She wasn't sure where the urgency, almost panic came from, but Cal had warriors train on the throwers. They had some of the firearms left behind by the peace between Congu and Sombi, but many had travelled across the river, and ammunition was an issue.

Ten days after the train broke through the barrier, the lookout whistled shrilly.

"Civilians to safety. Warriors to their posts. Send a runner to the Mtuaka's staal. Civilians carry everything they can, if we are forced to torch the village, they'll lose everything."

Soon they could see two boats chugging across the river, more barge than boat, but Cal expected they were full of soldiers. If they could get ashore, it would be a bloody battle, and she wasn't sure they could hold out despite ttaoku's optimism. She ran to the stable and built a fire under the boiler. There was a last-ditch surprise she could leave for the Kershians, but she hoped she didn't have to use it. She ran back out to ttaoku.

"The Kershians always underestimate the Sombi, and I expect they will the Congu."

"We can't count on the enemy's stupidity. Assume we're facing people who expect to fight hard."

"As you say," Ttaoku said. "Do we know the maximum range of the disc throwers?"

"The farther they go, the less effective they will be. A barrage at close range is our best chance."

The boats approached and rifle fire buzzed past them, Cal was glad she'd insisted on the barriers, even if they made the disc throwers more awkward to use. The smell of gunpowder wafted over them.

"Now," Cal shouted. The ten throwers snapped discs at the boats. Aim was by dragging the thrower to where they hoped it would point in a useful direction. None of the first shots hit a boat, though some were close enough to make a pause in the rifle fire. They loaded and fired again.

The first to hit made a hole in the side of the barge. Others flew close by or splashed in the water. They were intended to hit gigantic air ships, not relatively small barges.

Another struck near the hole and closer to the water, but fire from the barges intensified and warriors were dropping. Then a lucky shot blew a hole at water level on the second barge which soon wallowed through the water. It grounded not quite to the shore and the soldiers piled out, holding their rifles over their head. Congu fire dropped some and the discs were devastating but too slow to reload. The second boat grounded on the shore and more soldiers jumped over the side keeping a hail of bullets flying to pin the defenders down. Still, they put enough holes in the boat to be sure it wasn't going to return across the river.

With close to forty soldiers on shore, Cal spotted two more barges coming across the river. Even if the Mtuaka sent help it would be too late. She didn't have time to waver.

"Final barrage at the soldiers, then retreat, set the fires." Cal gave the order, then dashed for the staal. She had the boiler going at full pressure in the stable. She and ttaoku threw as much wood as they could on the fire and Cal jammed the safety pressure valve.

The retreat from kkittu was orderly. Cal'd made it clear she didn't want any heroes hanging back, the fires should keep the invaders busy while they escaped.

"Set up a sniper line," Ttaoku ordered; the rest switched to bow or spear. "Use the jungle to our advantage. We aren't going to stop them from taking kkittu, but we can stop them from moving to threaten the Mtuaka staal. Cal, you go with the wounded to the Mtuaka."

She was going to argue but thought better of it.

"Don't get killed." Cal followed the walking wounded through the jungle. Even from the jungle, the distant thud of the boiler failing hit her hard.

"It isn't over. Not by a long shot."

***

Llathia cursed the reeds. They were perfect for what she wanted, almost. The thinner ones were too flexible, the thicker too heavy. A test of the eagle was still a long way off.

"Llathia, a runner came into the village. Kkittu has fallen to the Kershians. The civilians escaped, but the warriors took significant casualties. They are holding the invaders for the moment." Hovid interrupted her tantrum.

"And the Anglian?"

"She is alive and uninjured. Word is the disc throwers she built were devastating when they hit."

"I want her here. Even if you have to drag her."

"Yes, my lady."

"And order the warriors to help hold the Kershians back. I don't want them moving any farther.

Llathia turned back to the reed. Maybe she should try more triangles. She was sure the Anglian would have an opinion. She wasn't sure if she wanted to listen yet.

***

Astrid looked out the window of the embassy. They'd been stuck waiting for what felt like forever, though it had only been a week.

"Let's go out and look around."

"It wouldn't be wise to be seen on the street." Pentam looked up from whatever he was writing.

"Not wise, but perhaps necessary," Bundo said. "We are hidden away safe from any watchers, but then we can't see them either. It is time to flush out the prey."

"And if you are the ones being hunted?" Pentam frowned.

"You can't hunt and stay safe," Astrid commented. "But knowing we're hunted gives us an advantage."

"True." Bundo nodded.

"You just want to go outside," Gretta said.

"Also true," Astrid admitted. "But I do think we will get nowhere if something isn't shaken up."

"And if you end up with a knife in the back?" Pentam's frown deepened.

"The best assassin in the Empire is tasked with my death. She is one of the few people my father fears. Sitting here is only delaying the inevitable."

"I see I won't be able to convince you, but at least take one of the guards with you as a guide and protection. I will send a note to the city guard."

"I can live with that." Astrid headed for the room she and Gretta had been given. "Let's get ready while Mr. Booksdale arranges our escort."

Zithaya wasn't just warmer than the Empire, it smelled different. Some undefinable spice floated in the air. If Astrid had been dropped blindfolded on the streets of Hanginj she would have known she was somewhere far from home.

"I would love to get some Zithayan clothes," Gretta said, "and I'd like to see the food market."

"As would I."

Their escort was a Zithayan guard, even with the exotic shape of his clothes, it was obvious he was in uniform.

"Is my duty to watch you." He spoke in heavily accented Anglian. Perhaps he didn't speak Kershian. They, after all, didn't speak Zithayan. He led them to an open carriage and they road that through the city. A few people stopped and pointed at the foreigners. Astrid restrained herself from waving back.

The market was packed with people. They weren't all dressed alike, nor did they look alike, but they mixed without apparent issue. Their guide stopped to talk to another guard at the entry to the market. The other man shrugged and waved them on.

Vendors sold everything from vegetables to spiders and scorpions on sticks, and other things less recognizable. They ate something from a stall the escort suggested. It was sweet and spicy, more vegetable than meat.

After two hours of wandering the market, Astrid was getting tired from watching the people so closely.

"Let's find a place to sit down for a bit," Gretta said as if reading Astrid's mind. They'd tacitly agreed to speak in Anglian to include their escort.

"Somewhere ahead, by a fountain," he said.

The fountain cooled the air and made Astrid realize she was thirsty. "I'm going to go over and get a drink of tea. Anyone else want one?"

"I'll come with you." Gretta followed Astrid to the tea stand that looked like every other one they'd seen. A hard blow pushed Astrid stumbling into Gretta. *This is it; this is where I die.* But other than a line of ice down her left arm, she felt fine.

Bundo held one man's wrist at an impossible angle, kicked another man. Their escort was down bleeding from a wound in his chest. A man in a mask charged at them with a knife, but a pot of tea shattered on his face.

He cursed in some language she didn't know and tore the mask off, the hate in his eyes palpable. Bundo's elbow connected with the back of the man's head and his eyes rolled up. Suddenly the square was filled with guards. Bundo stood between Astrid, Gretta and the crowd as the guards struck down attackers with clubs. The man from the tea stand came out and handed Astrid a cup. He bowed briefly and returned to his stall. Astrid sipped at the tea, but instead of calming her, it released her reaction to the point she had to hold the cup with both hands. She noticed blood dripping off her elbow.

Gretta's arm went around her waist and supported her as the world tilted.

***

Bundo kept scanning the square as the Zithayans were taking the surviving attackers into custody. Somebody would be watching, would report back that these foreigners were not the easy targets they had been told. But he couldn't spot them.

Astrid stood shaking while Gretta bandaged the cut on her arm.

"It is one thing to expect people to try to kill you, quite another for them to jump out of a peaceful crowd."

"Our apologies, Miss Czrmen." A member of the Zithayan guard came over. "The isolationists have been more active in recent years, any foreigner in Hanginj is a possible target." He glanced over at Bundo. "Good thing your friend is so vigilant."

"It isn't the first time he's saved me." Astrid took a long breath and exhaled her fear and uncertainty. She was an astonishing young woman. He hoped she survived to succeed in her plan, but Bundo's experience suggested this was only a test. Now that he'd revealed himself, they would adjust their actions. It would only take one person with a rifle. That wouldn't allow them to claim the assassination, so unless the people behind them grew impatient it would be people with knives and swords.

"Miss Czrmen, I have received a message to escort you to the government offices."

"When you're ready, officer." Astrid caught Bundo's eye and nodded at the man. Bundo raised an eyebrow slightly. He wouldn't be the first guardsman to work for the enemy. Hard to eliminate being in a position of trust. For now, Bundo would watch him closely, there was nothing else to do.

The guard led them out of the market, then turned down a narrow street. Bundo put his hand out to stop the girls.

"He's leading us the wrong way." He spoke in Kershian. The guard stiffened. "Go tell your masters we are watching, but take care, they don't like failure."

"How did you know he was going the wrong way?" Gretta asked.

"You need to know the ground to hunt."

"Makes sense."

"This way." Bundo led them away toward the embassy.

***

"The Kershian loyalists in Sombi have retaken control of the train corridor and coal mine. They have a foothold on the south shore of the Sombu river, but they are trapped for the moment." General Mizvrat reported to the emperor

"No matter." The emperor grinned. "They won't hold out against the Kershian army. Move ahead plans for the invasion. I want the Kershian flag flying over that god-forsaken country before summer."

"The fleet won't be ready." General Mizvrat stopped himself from sighing.

"What can they do to stop us?" The emperor flung himself into a chair. "We're invincible."

"We are technologically superior but hardly invincible. Strange things happen in war."

"You're just old, Mizvrat. Make it happen before summer or retire and let someone with better nerves take over."

General Mizvrat clenched his jaw, but this fool would appoint a bigger fool and the Empire would begin its slide into oblivion. "Four months."

"There that wasn't so hard. Nothing to be afraid of."

General Mizvrat saluted and stomped out of the office, not caring that it was his, not the Emperor's.

Chapter 10 Work is a Refuge

"Our village burned up." Kkitatin pouted. "All my nice clothes and everything."

"Clothes and even villages can be replaced." Lady Mtuaka said. "People cannot. I'm glad you are safe."

Cal wasn't sure if that extended to her. The invitation to move to the engine smith village wasn't very polite, nor something she could decline. For now, she'd let kkitatin do the talking.

"I hate them."

"Hate is a waste of energy." Lady Mtuaka frowned. "We must put our energy into pushing them back over the river, then out of Sombi."

"That might be harder than you think, and not because of their weapons. There are Kershians who were born and raised in Sombi. They'll be fighting for their homes." Cal sighed. "The Kershians aren't all bad, any more than the Sombi were when Congu and Sombi were enemies."

"If they fight us, they are enemies."

"And when they stop?" Cal rubbed her temples.

"I'll worry about it when they stop." Lady Mtuaka made it clear the discussion was over. "We don't have the luxury of time. You will begin building an airship tomorrow. I have a project I will be working on."

"What about me?" kkitatin crossed her arms.

"You can help Anda with the whirligigs." Lady Mtuaka pointed at Cal. "If you want to pursue a side hunt, talk to me first. Report to me each day on your progress."

"Aye." Cal saluted. "I would like to try to recover the engines from the barges we wrecked. I don't expect them to leave them there for us."

"You sound like you don't think they are staying."

"I wouldn't. Not with hostile snipers in the jungle, the village burned out and indefensible. If they hang around our snipers will pick them off. I don't think they have eighty soldiers to throw away. I hope they don't."

"Very well, if you can recover the engines, do so, but don't put anyone at risk doing it."

***

"They took their wounded and dead and left before the fires burned out." Ttaoku pointed to the remains of the village. "Couldn't see if they took the other boats, but I don't think so, they were in too much of a rush to get out of there."

"No sign of action from the village."

"It is deserted. Ddokna led some warriors through the village to check. Didn't think to ask him to check the boats."

"Let's go then."

The reek of smoke made Cal's head ache. She put a cloth over her mouth and nose to cut the smell. At least there were no bodies.

At first glance, the grounded barge looked like a lost cause, but closer inspection showed that the damage was superficial.

"Bring the wagon up." Cal waved them forward. She looked in the stable for her tools and found most of them, black with soot, but solid enough. Some of the pipe had survived as well. "Scavenge everything you can from the stable. If it is metal, bring it, except for the pieces of the boiler." Then she jumped into the boat and started dismantling the engine and boiler. They loaded the wagon with all the parts they could lift. The lifting arm on the wagon strained to lift the boiler, but it held. Cal admired the simple efficiency of the design.

"We're done here, let's take all this back to Lady Mtuaka." Cal stared regretfully at the sunken boat, but they weren't going to reach it today.

***

"First thing is we need a ship." Cal tossed a bit of the giant reed in her hand. "If we can build it out of this, we can save a lot of weight and time. We're going to build a cage first. Big enough to hold the engines and a few people." She outlined the size she wanted on the ground. "Use the biggest ones to form the rectangle."

"Yes, Cal." Hovid turned and started instructing the rest of the team in rapid Congu. They laid out the reeds. Cal had someone carve logs to put inside the hollow reeds at the joins to add strength.

The Congu lashed everything together with rope made from jungle vines. The work went faster than Cal expected and by the end of the day, they had a wobbly box.

"You need to use triangles for strength." Lady Mtuaka demonstrated on one corner.

"You're right." Cal shook her head; she should have thought of that. She wasn't thinking like an engineer. "I'll need some longer pieces of the larger stuff to build the base for the floor."

"I will let them know." Lady Mtuaka sent Anda up in the balloon to pass on the message. With her broken arm, she couldn't do much more than be a messenger and work with the young people from the staal on the whirligigs.

"They said they'd have some tomorrow evening," Anda reported when she finally landed.

"What are you using to control the buoyancy? Cal couldn't think of the Congu word. "How much it floats."

"I slowly let the fire out. Too quickly and the balloon crashes." She waved her splinted arm.

"I developed a system that will be more efficient." She lifted the top of the envelope. "We put a flap in here and control it with two ropes."

"I don't know. I'll have to ask the engine smith."

"Let me know what she says." Cal headed back over to the rectangle, now much less fragile looking.

"We get the longer pieces we need tomorrow. I'd rather not have joints in the floor if we can avoid them. While we wait, we'll need to get the wood to build platforms for the boilers and engines, something strong and light. Strong is essential."

Hovid talked with a couple of men from the team, and they went off into the jungle. Cal shrugged.

"The rest of you, collect the short pieces of the reed, I have an idea of how to use them. I need to go find Lady Mtuaka."

"Lady Mtuaka…"

"Engine Smith," she said. "Here I am the engine smith."

"Engine Smith, then." Cal rubbed her head. "I have an idea to use the shorter pieces of the reed to make steam cannon. Like guns, but with steam powering them, not gunpowder."

"I know what a cannon is."

"May I use the time waiting for the next lot of reeds to experiment?"

"Yes, they don't take a lot of interior pressure. I tried to use them in the steam engine, it was a disaster. Good thing Hovid had us all standing well back."

"Yes." Cal headed off back to work, thinking about how to safely test the steam cannon.

***

Llathia watched Cal walk back to work. She had to admit the Anglian knew what she was doing and was good at it. What she'd give to have the talent Cal had. Llathia was planning to use the reeds to build her eagle, but would she have thought to use the large pieces to build the frame for the ship? Maybe she should have asked the woman's advice.

No, she had to do this herself. She was the engine smith.

The problem she was having was the larger the wings, the more unstable they were. Llathia closed her eyes and imagined the eagles flying but couldn't bring a solution to mind. Maybe they were moving their wings, but not enough for her to see.

Llathia headed for the balloon, she could go up now, and come down in the morning with the reeds. She thought of Anda's crash. There had to be a better way to control the descent. Cal had built a ship, she'd know.

"Come and help me get the balloon going. I want to go up top."

"Chiza's up there, isn't he?" Divoj asked as they spread the cloth out.

"He is, but so are the eagles."

When the balloon was almost full, Llathia climbed and stirred the fire. There was something about floating up that was relaxing. Her worries stayed on the ground, waiting for her to return in the morning.

When Chiza's strong arms lifted her out of the basket, llathia wrapped her arms around him and kissed him.

"It hasn't been that many days since you saw me." His gentle rumbling voice caressed her.

"I'm having trouble getting the larger eagle to fly. The whirligigs are the same, after a certain size they don't work the same way.

"You'll figure it out." He hugged her then stepped back. "You are staying the night, I hope?"

"Oh yes." Heat invaded her face and she buried it in his chest, then reluctantly moved away. "I need to watch the eagles some more."

Calliope and the Engine Smith

They sat side by side watching the huge birds. The eagles floated effortlessly mocking her with their grace. One folded its wings and plummeted like a stone.

"Supper time," Chiza said. "They see birds we can't, but I don't often see them come back up without something to eat."

Something reared up in the back of llathia's mind. She froze for fear of losing it. Another eagle dropped to hunt, and it came in the light.

"Weight balance," Llathia whispered. "They need the weight between their wings to add stability. I've been keeping the weight down as much as possible." She jumped to her feet, but Chiza pulled her down.

"Morning is soon enough."

***

Cal watched the bundle of reeds grow float down from a safe vantage point. Using the balloon to move materials was a brilliant solution.

The engine smith clambered out of the basket as the team expertly took up the envelope to keep it from the brazier. She smiled at Cal, but Cal's head twinged, and she rubbed her temples. Something was off, but she didn't know what it was. There was no fever, no nausea. She tried a smile but was too slow and the engine smith's face closed off again.

"That should keep you busy." She walked away, obliviously already thinking of something else.

"Okay, let's get to work." Cal suppressed a sigh. "We've got a lot to do and not much time."

They put cross beams from corner to corner of the rectangle, Hovid expertly fitting the crossing point to be flat.

"We should put a layer of beams the long way, then smaller ones across the other way." One of the women waved her hands in illustration.

"Sounds good. You're in charge." Cal's headache was getting worse by the second. Suddenly the world went off plumb and Cal fell to the ground. She dug her fingers in to keep from falling off as the ground spun around her.

"Cal!" Hovid ran over. "What happened?"

Cal tried to explain, but the words came out in a jumble of Kershian, Anglian and Congu. Tears ran down her face and she couldn't stop them

"Fetch the engine smith and see if there is a healer in the village."

The world's tilting didn't slow, and Cal began to panic. The team held her in place. Gravity still worked properly for them. Then the pain spiked like a nail had been driven into her skull. She screamed and dove gratefully into unconsciousness.

Chapter 11 What is Precious

Kkitatin paced outside the house where the healer sat with Cal, chanting monotonously. No one was allowed in the house but him and Cal.

Llathia went to work at the cave to work so kkitatin was left to keep watch. Her father would be worried, but he wasn't here to worry, so she'd worry for him. It was her duty as First Daughter.

Being First Daughter was nothing like kkitatin had imagined. Her father was as busy as the King of Sombi, he'd brought home this pale woman and announced she was his First Wife. The woman knew but a few words of Congu, and nothing of custom. She enraged kkitatin at first. Then she was interesting. The things she built, like those disc throwers and that flying machine. Kkitatin was angry it had crashed before she got a ride in it.

Now the woman lay silent with the healer chanting death away. The chanting slowed and stopped. The healer came out of the house, wiping his hands dry.

"I have done what I can. It is in her hands and yours." He put a hand on her shoulder. "Talk to her, keep her room cheery. I will come each day to change the bandages. Try to get her to drink broth, but be careful, you don't want her to choke."

"What happened?" She wanted to run to Cal's side but also stay here safely outside.

"She had pressure in her head. I've relieved the pressure, but I don't know at what cost." He patted her shoulder and pushed

88

her toward the house. "Just do what you can and pray it will be enough. It is all any of us can do."

Kkitatin sat in the room staring at the motionless woman. What was she supposed to talk about?

"King vvatha just thought I was a nuisance. He tried to give me away as a bride. My father asked me what I wanted, and llathia came up with the idea of the adoption…"

Kkitatin talked about how lonely it was with her father away. How hard she worked to get a staal her father could be proud of. She talked until her throat was dry.

"Time to try feeding you some broth."

***

"All hands to your stations!" Commander Harkness bellowed. "Pump out the ballast." Water splashed in the tiny ship as the crew dashed to save the ship. The lamps flickered and smoked making Commander Harkness cough.

"We continue to sink." Samantha reported, "we are below the test depth. Suggest we use full power ahead with the fins aligned to bring us to the surface."

"Are we clear of obstacles?"

"Aye, commander."

"Full ahead, fins to surfacing position."

The underwater ship careened forward. The level on the bridge said they were pointed up, but whether they were actually climbing was a different thing.

"Commander we're approaching the surface, no ships in the immediate vicinity."

"Get the hoses ready, as soon as we hit the surface, get them out the hatch and we pump like mad."

At first, Commander Harkness was sure they were taking on more water than they were pumping out, then Samantha called out. 'Positive buoyancy.'

"Let's dry the ship out, then get back to port, we have a lot of work to do."

***

Astrid and Gretta looked at the invitation printed on a heavy card.

"Looks like we'll get to meet the Secretary, she's invited us and Mr. Booksdale. Tomorrow afternoon at two." Gretta flapped the card.

"Fantastic, I'm getting cabin fever sitting here."

"Bundo has a point, it is very risky to be out about town. Especially since we need to let the guard know when and where we will be.

They dressed up as best they could the next day and rode with Mr. Booksdale to the Secretary's office. Bundo rode on top with the driver keeping a close watch. The carriage pulled up in front of the office without incident and guards escorted them into the building.

The Secretary welcomed them into what must have been the Zithayan equivalent of a drawing room.

"I thought it best to meet informally." She poured tea for them. "Zithayan formality is hard enough for us who grew up with it.

"You are too kind," Astrid said.

"How can one be too kind?" The secretary looked over at Mr. Booksdale.

"It is an expression, meaning one is being extra kind," he explained.

"Curious."

"I am told you are a member of the Kershian Royal family." She returned her gaze to Astrid. "Perhaps you can explain why your people are funding the isolationists."

"I am not part of the government, Secretary, but I would guess that Kershia would prefer Zithaya to be internally involved and uninterested in what is occurring elsewhere."

"Locossia is far away from us."

"With steam engines and airships, the world is getting smaller. That is, it takes less time to travel from one place to another."

"True, we have learned such from our discussions with the Anglians. Is Kershia planning to ask for our friendship too?"

"Not Kershia, me." Astrid sipped at her tea. "I plan to charge the emperor with incompetence, if the charges are upheld, I will be in line for the throne. It would be good to have Zithaya's approval of me as a leader."

"We can hardly approve of something we have never seen."

"When you have seen, then. I want peace and believe it is possible, but only if Kershia pays more attention to what is happening at home than on taking over the rest of the world."

Astrid nibbled on a biscuit. "Trading is one thing but taking over other countries' government and resources is criminal."

"I would agree yet stepping in to stop such would require us to enter the very war we wish to avoid."

"I am not asking you to step in. It is an internal Kershian matter, and I would not sink my people into civil war."

"Will your Emperor stand aside peacefully?"

"I will need to convince the military and the nobility that what he is doing is bad for the country."

"That will be a difficult task, and one we cannot aid you in." The Secretary frowned slightly.

"I understand." Astrid pushed down her disappointment, even though she'd expected no less.

"We will be watching you with interest, princess, but I would prefer to watch from a greater distance."

"I believe there will be a ship in Puhkan to take us away."

"I heard about the attack on you in the market. I will place a group of my personal guard to escort you safely to port."

Outside, they climbed into the carriage.

"Where do you plan to go?" Mr. Booksdale asked.

"It depends on what ships are there and what money we have for passage."

"I will get Ambassador Strathes to write you a letter to get you to Anglia."

"It would be nice to see my father again, but I expect other people will think the same thing." Astrid took a shuddering breath. "It was nice to meet you."

Mr. Strathes saw them off personally, He shook Astrid's hand and left a tiny bit of paper in it. When they'd started off, she read the note. *Trust Uncle John.*

Strange. She didn't have an Uncle John. The note must be part of some cloak and dagger business.

The carriage ride to Puhkan was long and the sea voyage would be longer. Time enough to think about it then.

An Anglian ship was in port. They boarded and presented a letter from Mr. Strathes to the captain.

"We can always use more maids." The captain said and waved over the purser. "Get these girls uniforms, they will be working off their voyage.

"Aye, sir." The purser guided them away as if picking up strays in all corners of the world was normal. Perhaps it was.

Bundo took a job in the engineering room on the ship.

***

Roger bit back the angry reply he wanted to make

"It is true the Kershians have moved in Sombi." He made his voice calm. "That doesn't mean they can't be pushed back again."

"They have guns, engines, machines. How will we stand against them?" leRash waved his arms.

"Each soldier carries a gun and ammunition. Kill that soldier, and we have the gun and ammunition. They are not invincible; arrows and spears will hurt them. A tree across the track held their machines back for months. The Kershians are as human as we are."

"Not according to them." leRash said. "Each of their 'outposts' is the same. Fortified, defended by guns and cannon. Deny them what they want, and they'd slaughter every one of us and not think twice. What will they do if we fight a war against them?"

"It won't matter," Phil'kc said. "They will knock us down one at a time or all together. The Kershians rule the desert kingdom in all but name. Do we bow our necks or fight for freedom?"

"We fight together, we are strong." Roger stood. "When they come for Sombi, where are their closest troops? You don't need to fight in Sombi, fight in your own countries. They are ants, without the queen they are just things to step on. Their strength is also their weakness."

"We will watch events in Sombi." leRash nodded. "It costs nothing to be ready."

***

Cal fought the sea serpent trying to cut Pentam free, but the seaweed grabbed at her, cut at her. Cal fought free. Then she was wrestling fire and smoke. pieces of roofing fell on her and trapped her. She screamed, then it was a mountain crushing her. Her head was in agony.

Then it stopped, leaving her floating in a peaceful darkness. She wouldn't mind spending eternity here.

Something warm touched her lips, a familiar taste. Whenever she was sick, her mother made broth from chicken bones for her. Cal reached for the taste and opened her eyes.

A beautiful young black girl held a spoon, her eyes wide.

"Cal, you're awake." The words echoed in her mind. She tried to say something in response, but the words wouldn't come. Instead, she took the spoon and bowl the girl was holding and started eating the broth.

Kkitatin, the name came to her with the last of the broth.

"Kkitatin, thank you." Words and memory flooded into her mind then settled into a semblance of order. "What happened?"

"You collapsed building the airship. The healer said you had pressure in your head."

"I remember the headaches." Cal took stock. "My head still hurts, but it is different."

"The healer had to relieve the pressure."

"Makes sense." Cal leaned back. "Explains why I'm so…"

Chapter 12 Recovery

A week after she woke, Cal staggered out of the house she'd been in; cared for by kkitatin the entire time. Her balance was still off, so she used a stick to lean on as she walked to the cave. Kkitatin, who'd appointed herself Cal's keeper, kept careful watch. A kerchief covered Cal's partly shaved head and protected her from the sun's heat.

"I know they've been busy, but I haven't been able to check in days."

"I appreciate your dedication." Cal put a hand on the girl's shoulder to keep her balance.

"You okay?" She looked up at Cal.

"I am." Cal waited for the dizzy spell to pass. They were getting shorter, but no less unpredictable.

In the clearing in front of the cave, the body of the airship was complete, large smokestacks rising from the boilers.

"Good, you're here. We're putting in the engines." The engine smith helped Cal through the opening. "We have two engines. We're thinking a bow and stern propeller system."

"Two of things is smart." Cal couldn't find the word she wanted. "You are using the whirligigs to design the props?"

"They gave us our first model. Hovid has been tweaking the shape. He suggested putting one out each side to give us steering." The engine smith pointed to holes in the walls.

"That would work. Are you using two envelopes too? It would make losing a balloon less catastrophic."

"That's the plan. We're building in the valves in the envelope you told Anda about."

"Valves?" Cal wrinkled her forehead. "Oh, the buoyancy flaps in the balloon. Yes, that's a good idea.

Cal walked to the cave each day, then home exhausted. The more tired she got, the more she struggled with words, to the point she found a board and charcoal to draw out what she was trying to say.

Kkitatin hovered around her, bringing a stool from the village for her to sit on. Replacing charcoal sticks and fetching water.

"The healer told me to watch over you." She said when Cal asked about it. They used all the fabric they could find for the balloons and asked for more.

Cal spent her time working on the disc throwers, she figured out a way to make them spin, which more than doubled their range. They would never be as accurate as cannon, but she was sure they could hit another air ship. When she wasn't building weapons or the airship, she went over battle scenarios in her mind.

How do we train for a battle that has never been fought before?

***

Llathia had to admit the Anglian woman was impressive. Back to work only a week after she was at death's door. They were making astonishing progress on the airship. The cabin was all but complete with windows to fire the discs through and a back double door she had her own plans for. The work on the airship and Cal's illness had put the eagle glider off to the side, but llathia spent spare moments imagining soaring high above the ground.

The day came to test the first envelope. They used the brazier from the up and down balloon to heat the air. All day they kept the fire burning to fill the envelope, find a seam that split, fix that and fill the envelope again.

"How are we going to keep the airship up?" llathia asked as the pile of firewood shrank. "All the weight will be taken with wood to burn."

"I have an idea about that, but it will be a risk. We need to get the ship operational to pull it off."

"What are you thinking?"

"We take the coal mine. Coal creates more heat for weight than wood."

"The Kershians have many soldiers, and they are rumoured to use forced labour in the mine."

"And I would guess that they used most of them to take Kkittu. They had four boats; we sank two of them. We caused some casualties in the battle. Ttaoku sent a runner to say the Kershians had carried twenty people onto the boat, it still took two trips with each remaining boat, so I'd guess they had about sixty healthy soldiers after the battle."

"The warriors from Sombi report a similar number." Llathia shook her head. "We'll need more warriors than that if we are going to take them on head-to-head."

"We have the Sombi and the Congu warriors together, and I don't plan on taking them on in a pitched battle."

"You don't plan to take them on…" Llathia's voice went hard.

"Sorry, you'll be in command as Lady Mtuaka, but as the only person with time flying airships, I have some ideas about how to use that to our advantage."

"I see." Llathia sat in silence until the last of the anger flowed away. "I am the engine smith. I've built engines to run smithies and sawmills. We have a wagon that crawls at the speed of my walk. But everything that I've built, you've already made. I feel like a girl before her hunt taking on a seasoned warrior."

"I can imagine that would be hard, but you're wrong on two counts." Cal held up a finger. "I never imagined in my wildest dreams building a boiler and engine parts from wood. You not only made it work, but you are also actively using them for industry. The second thing is, I didn't personally build everything. I had a team of good people like you have, and they did most of the work."

"You are just saying that." Llathia hated the whine in her voice.

"I don't just say things, Lady Mtuaka. We are equals, at least when it comes to engineering. You are taking care of a much bigger clan than I ever had to at the same time."

"First Wife is handling the clan."

"She can only do that because you kept it in good shape for her. Having the children play with the whirligigs is genius, what a great way to test the concept."

"I want to build something to glide like an eagle," Llathia said. "But I'm scared, what if I fail?"

"Engineering is all about failing safely, then improving the design, failing again, and improving the design."

"How do you fail safely with something like the eagle?" Llathia's heart sank, she was further from soaring in the sky than she'd thought.

"Build the one you think you can fly in, then throw it off the cliff with a log tied in where you would be. Watch it all the way down. You don't put yourself into the glider until you are sure you will survive."

"Hovid told me you said something about making your mistakes survivable."

"Won't be much good as an engineer, or a hunter if you don't take care to stay alive." Cal grinned crookedly.

"You keep saying *engineer*. What does it mean?" llathia frowned.

"It is the Anglian way of saying engine smith."

"Well, I'm glad you are here, engineer Cal."

"Call me Cal." The Anglian women looked open and friendly. Maybe llathia had misjudged her.

"Call me llathia, then." Llathia smiled. "Let's talk about this battle plan of yours."

Chapter 13 A Meeting of Sisters

"So that's Anglia." Astrid pointed at the line in the distance.

"That would make sense." Gretta stretched and groaned. "We have twelve more cabins to make up and check for left-behind belongings."

"I didn't expect working to be so…"

"Exhausting?"

"Fulfilling." Astrid put a hand on her friend's shoulder. "It is nice to be wanted for something more than one's name. Let's see if we can finish the cabins in time to watch the ship come into port."

"We'd better if we're supposed to re-unite passengers with their belongings."

They had the routine down after weeks at sea. Gretta found a diamond ring in one cabin, which earned her a nice tip from the new bride.

They got off the ship with a bonus in their pockets, saying farewell to Bundo who planned to continue on to visit his sister in Ferandica. "I will bring more attention to you than would be healthy."

"We should take the train to the capital," Gretta said, counting money in her hand. "A cab will take up all our spare cash."

"Train is fine with me." Astrid pointed at the crowd marching like a parade toward the railway station. "But let's take the next one, this one will be full of former passengers."

They stopped in a pub and had fish and chips with tea, much to the dismay of the owner who believed everyone should enjoy at least a pint of beer at his establishment.

A stranger slid in beside Gretta. "Brilliant idea to meet here, girls."

"And who might you be?" She asked sliding farther along the bench.

"My name would be meaningless to you, but you can call me Uncle John. Your sister sent me to fetch you safely."

"I am none the wiser."

"Mr. Strathes sent a message saying you'd be visiting." He put a card on the table, the handwriting looked like Mr. Strathes' who penned a letter to the captain of whatever Anglian ship happened to be in port.

Astrid pulled out the letter to compare.

"This chap bothering you?" The pub owner frowned at him. "Don't hold with anyone bothering the young ladies."

"It is all right." Gretta smiled at the man. "We were just startled, didn't expect Uncle John to meet us at the port."

"All good, then." The man smiled broadly. "Your meal will be out in a few minutes."

"So Uncle John, do you meet all your nieces?" Astrid turned back to her meal to finish while it was still hot.

"Your sister was very insistent. She worried about two girls alone in a port town."

"So meeting in a pub might be a problem." Gretta sipped her tea.

"She'd approve of the tea."

"How is Aunt Joan?" Astrid asked.

"Looking forward to seeing you again. I'll warn you she's been baking for two days."

Gretta and Astrid took turns asking about fictional relatives and learned that Great-Uncle Harold was suffering from an onset of gout, probably from too much brandy, and that Cousin Will was doing well enough at school. When Uncle John had finished his meal and his pint, they sauntered out of the pub and down to the railway station. He produced three tickets and the woman at the wicket waved them through.

"Next train in an hour."

Astrid stayed silent as Gretta and Uncle John chatted. This was a very different welcome from Zithaya, and it suggested they weren't much safer in Anglia. *I wonder what feeling safe is like? If I do take the throne, I'll never find out.*

The train pulled in with puffs of steam and after the passengers disembarked, the trio climbed on board and settled in a berth.

"We should have finagled some luggage," Astrid said. "It will look odd for us not to have any."

"I told the porter you'd sent it on ahead. You didn't want to wrestle with the steam trunks."

"Very good." Gretta clapped her hands. "Though I wish we did have steamer trunks."

"It was good thinking to quiz me on the family. The owner didn't relax until we shared family stories."

"Thanks, I guess. We were just pulling your leg." Astrid frowned. "Just how high is the danger level here? Are there groups like the isolationists who can be conned into doing the work of my other uncle?"

"Sadly, there are always people whose love of money outweighs any conscience they might have once had." Uncle John shook his head. "It has been arranged for you to attend a rather exclusive school for girls. It would be all but impossible to plant someone there without us knowing about it. People keep trying, but the screening of every employee from janitor to principal is taken exceptionally seriously, and you will have a maid as well."

"And how long will we be at this school?" Astrid frowned. "Our last school might have been described in similar terms."

"Which makes it not all that surprising that rumour says you burned it down." Uncle John dropped the jovial façade. "The nieces and nephews of the Crown Prince, plus a fair number of Admiralty children attend. You'll be in good company."

"I'm not sure if that is reassuring or makes me more nervous." Gretta shivered.

"Your cover story is you are distant cousins of her Majesty. Do you mind being sisters for a while?"

"I actually am a distant cousin of your queen," Astrid said. "Some of my ancestors were known for being prolific, if not wise."

"All the better then. Some of the students are very into genealogy, you'll be able to assuage their interest."

"Lovely." Gretta rolled her eyes. "We'd better be careful with our story."

"There is an Astrid about my age who is the daughter of a cadet branch of the Royal Family. Important enough to be impressive and dull enough to be safe." Astrid sighed. "She is a very pleasant girl and not at all interested in politics."

The remainder of the trip was spent drumming the few family names which might get asked about into Gretta's head.

An ordinary carriage picked them up from the station along with their fictional steamer trunks.

"I know you must be getting tired, but the principal would like to meet with you before you go to your room." Uncle John looked out the window at the passing houses.

"Does the principal know the truth?" Astrid closed her eyes.

"She does, but then she works for the same people I do."

"Right." Astrid pinched the bridge of her nose. "Who else knows?"

"No one at the school. You will be a bit unusual, but not unique."

The carriage pulled through the gates to an impressive building that had to be the school.

"Come with me," Uncle John said. "The school staff will deal with your luggage." He led them inside and up a grand staircase, then along the hall to the right, stopping at a door with no nameplate. He knocked twice, then entered. Astrid and Gretta followed him in.

The first things Astrid noticed were the guards in the corner. The woman behind the desk looked the part of the principal of a girl's school. The other woman sat on a settee. She looked at Astrid but didn't stand, though the principal did.

"Welcome to Anglia, Astrid Tsalivrz."

"Thank you, Your Majesty." Astrid bowed while Gretta dropped into a deep curtsy. "It is good of you to welcome us personally."

"We needed to see for ourselves what kind of person you were."

"I understand."

"Do you?"

"You need to be as sure as possible the pretender to the Imperial throne is not a naïve girl with her head in the clouds."

"Very well then. Sit and we will chat for a few minutes." The queen pointed at the chairs across from her. "Tell us your goals for the Empire."

"We are wasting money and people on warmongering." Astrid perched on the chair. "I would like to see us focus more on trade. It will bring longer-term prosperity and broaden our horizons. We don't need to rule the world to be part of it."

"You think you can change the course of the empire just like that?"

"Yes, I do." Astrid met the old queen's gaze. "If I didn't, what would be the purpose? It won't be easy, nor quick, but that is my plan."

"Very well. What is your take on the empire's present action?"

"Shortsighted, crude, but not surprising given the personality of my uncle. Beyond that, I won't say anything to set off the war I'm trying to stop. I have plans in place to embarrass my uncle and set up the possibility of a competency trial. It is not my place to speak for other sovereign nations."

"So what is Anglia's part in your plan?"

"I would like Anglia's recognition as ruler of the Empire, should I succeed in the trial."

"Not before?" The queen raised an eyebrow slightly.

"I do not want civil war."

"You really think you can overturn the emperor without a war?"

"It's been done before." Astrid lifted her chin. "Historically I have a fifty/fifty chance."

The queen laughed. "We believe you are worth supporting. If you can do what you say, Anglia will be the first to support you. It will not happen with just wishful thinking. You will need to plan a political coup much more difficult than the civil war you want to avoid."

"I have a list of the nobility the emperor distrusts enough to hold their children hostage, and people who can discreetly suggest a ruler who doesn't hold families prisoner would be in their favour."

"If there is a way in which we may help within the constraints you have set yourself, let us know." The queen nodded in clear dismissal. Astrid stood and bowed.

"I will show you to your room." The principal stood. "If you would excuse me, Your Majesty."

Chapter 14 The Third Prince

Roger stopped at his father's kraal.

"Greetings, father."

"Good to see you, Roger. How did the conference go?"

"About as I expected. Interest, but a lot of caution. Kershia already has a lot of interests on our continent. They will not give them up easily."

"So no swarms of warriors ready to push the Kershians out of Harasah." The king smiled wryly.

"They will watch and learn from our success or defeat."

"What is the plan for success?"

"Surprise," Roger said. "They are expecting us to be cowed by their technology. I don't expect they will actually invade Sombi as much as take over Biafa, then rule as they did before, through the person on the throne. That means we can concentrate our forces on Biafa, though it won't be enough to defend the city. We need to send the Kershians home with their tails between their legs."

"You don't have much time. Kershian isn't making a big secret of their intention to punish Sombi for the massacre of Kershian citizens. The newest guess is at least three airships, as many warships and troop carriers. The emperor is impatient."

"We will need to call up warriors from the other clans." Roger sighed. "Mtuaka won't be an issue, but I can see some foot-dragging from the other clans."

"That's why I'm not asking them." The king grinned wickedly. "This will be a Mtuaka and Xanichi hunt and we will claim the glory of the hunt."

"Leaving the other clans to beg to be allowed to join." Roger laughed. "Pass the word to King vvatha, the Sombi in the east will need to be ready to rise."

"I believe the king has his own plans." The King shrugged. "He hasn't been forthcoming other than to welcome us to come and fight."

"That does sound like him. I will send a letter to ssyache, and we'll work out a way to coordinate on the ground."

"Very good." The king sobered. "You've heard about Kkittu?"

"The other nations were intent on rubbing it in my face to show the foolishness of fighting the Kershians. Are they still holding the shore?"

"Your wife figured they were coming, built defences, sunk two of their boats and from all accounts sent a quarter of the invaders home wounded. Then they torched the village and the staal and anything else that would burn. It left the Kershians with an undefendable position. They went back across the river before nightfall."

"There is a good reason the Anglians made her admiral over their air navy."

"Apparently." The king leaned forward. "Your First Wife was sick, collapsed out of nowhere. Latest orders for goods came with her signature, so she's alive, but I don't know much more than that."

"She's tough."

"She's married to you, she'd better be." The king laughed and leaned back. "I won't keep you from going to see her, but I'm sending warriors with you to be sure you arrive. The Kershians still have two boats and they may attack across the river again."

***

The villages they passed hadn't changed from the last time Roger had passed through. The young warriors were mostly off fighting, though it was the Kershians instead of the Sombi. The complaints weren't about the need for guns, but dissatisfaction with Lady Mtuaka. She had unreasonable expectations of the villages saying they needed to work in exchange for help with food. They'd rather have the young people back. A lot of the complaints started with 'In my day…"

Roger listened to them all, then replied the same way. The king had appointed Lady Mtuaka and would not interfere with how she ruled the clan. The people weren't happy, but he pointed out it wasn't her job to make them happy.

Concern for Cal made him ride past the turn-off to Kkittu to the Mtuaka staal, where First Wife greeted him.

"How did the conference go?"

"Much as I expected; lots of talk."

First Wife shook her head.

"The world won't be changed by talk."

"We have to start somewhere. Not long ago, it would have been spears on the battlefield. Talk is a step forward."

In the morning he ordered the soldiers escorting him to aid ttaoku watch Kkittu and scout up and down the shore to watch for Kershian activity, then he travelled on to the engine smith's village. From there it was a short walk to the cave. A person from the village guided him.

He'd never visited the cave before, so he expected something like Cal's workshop, maybe a bit bigger. The scale of the airship took his breath away. The balloon towered into the air, reaching almost halfway up the cliff. The ship part was bigger than some of the chieftains' huts in the villages.

"Father!" kkitatin called and ran over to him. "You're back safe."

"I am, my queen."

"We burned our town, but it meant the Kershians couldn't live there."

"We will rebuild." Roger put a hand on her shoulder.

"I already have ideas."

"I would be happy to hear them, but first, where is Cal?"

"I'll take you there." Kkitatin grabbed his hand and pulled him toward the ship. "She's supervising getting the engine ready to attach the props."

Cal sat on a stool pointing to things and talking in mixed Congo and Anglian, but the people moved as if they understood her.

"Roger." Cal stood up, then paused for a long breath before walking over to him. "It is good to see you."

"I hear you led the defence of Kkittu. The king was impressed."

"I wish we could have turned them away, but there were too many of them with guns. I denied them a foothold on the Congu side of the river, but the village was the cost."

"I approve. Easier to rebuild the village than push enemies out of our own staal."

"What news do you have for us?" Cal put a hand on kkitatin's shoulder as if to balance.

"We can't expect hordes of warriors from across Harasah, but the King is calling up all the Mtuaka and Xanichi warriors, and he has a plan to get warriors from the other clans too."

"Our first goal must be to retake the north shore of the Sombu river."

"I'm guessing you have a plan." Roger smiled.

"Llathia and I have discussed some ideas." Cal paused for a few heartbeats. "We'd be happy to have your input."

"The main thing is that the Kershians appear to be planning their invasion three months from now."

"I wouldn't think that would be the kind of thing they would advertise."

"Apparently they have so low an opinion of us they don't care if we know. A messenger has been sent to King vvatha who has his own ideas of how to defend Biafa."

"Three months," Cal sighed. "The first ship I built took a year, and it wasn't armed. We're working with a new design and a lot of unknowns. Don't have a choice, we'll make it happen."

"It looks impressive already."

"We need to make and test the second envelope, do power tests on the engine. The props haven't been tried yet… Sorry, I need to sit down."

"Are you all right to be working?" Roger followed her to the stool.

"As long as I don't overdo it. I'm getting stronger."

"You keep overdoing it," Kkitatin said, hands on her hips.

"True." Cal looked over the engine. "Looks good. Kkitatin, could you ask the engine smith to come and give it a look?"

Lady Mtuaka came over and peered at the engine, nodding to herself, making an adjustment here and there.

"Good work." She stretched. "I say we let the balloon deflate and work on engine two tomorrow."

***

"I think we're ready for our first tethered test." Llathia glanced over at Cal. The woman was right, they each had their strengths.

"Let's load up the ballast and start the balloons filling."

By noon the balloons towered over the clearing, filling out and pulling at the ropes. The ship creaked but held.

"Okay, we're good for the next part." Llathia climbed into the ship, followed by Chiza who'd insisted on being part of the test. "Push the ballast bags off, one at a time until the ship lifts, we just need it off the ground today."

The test went perfectly, the ship lifting a lot more weight than Cal expected.

"That's good. The more ballast we have, the more maneuverable the ship will be in the up and down direction. The propellers will give us steering. The ballast can act as a weapon too."

The next day they took the ship as high as the top of the cliff before lowering it.

"I like the ballast, when we started dropping too quickly, Chiza could push off a bag or two and slow the descent." Llathia couldn't help her broad smile

"They are very impressive when they hit the ground too. I wouldn't want to be too near one when it landed."

"Let's take her up and down a few more times this week. Shake her up and make sure she holds together." Llathia looked up at the cliff. "We'll start training people on the controls."

Chapter 15 First Cruise

"These are the props?" Cal tried to hide the dismay in her voice. They were large, ungainly things made of reeds and fabric.

"They are what we have," Llathia growled at her, and Cal stuffed her misgivings deep into her gut.

"Well, let's test them and see how they do." Cal and llathia double-checked the mountings. Llathia exuded confidence, and by the time they were ready for the test flight, Cal's nerves had settled.

There would be six people on this flight, one on each engine, two warriors to manage the ballast, llathia in command, and Cal observing.

Cal breathed steadily as the ship lifted from the ground. The reeds creaked but held. The boilers hissed, releasing pressure.

"Engines ahead one quarter," Llathia called. The props spun and stayed together. "Starboard engine ahead another notch. Hold it there, we're travelling straight... rising steady. Port engine back two notches."

Cal watched out an attack window as they travelled in a slow circle.

"Engines one-quarter reverse," Llathia called, and they slowed to a halt. "Holding over clearing. Descending. Warriors on ballast, hold." The ship crunched to the ground, but the reeds flexed, absorbing the energy. "Make fast. Hold the balloons for deflation."

Over the next week, they took the Flying Elephant, as kkitatin named it, up every day trying more complex maneuvers

116

and pushing the engines and props to the limits of their performance. Each day the team would check them over and make minor repairs. Cal began to relax.

***

"We're ready for a proper shakedown cruise," Cal said.

"I want to take it far enough south to get some proper height." Llathia stared into the distance. "Height is going to be important in air warfare."

"How so?"

"Imagine if you can get over the other airship. There is nothing they can do; they may not even know you're there. You could board their ship and take it over."

"That would take some planning and training, but it's an intriguing idea. I've been thinking about bringing them down and taking them out of the battle, but if you could take a ship, you could turn it against the enemy."

"I'm thinking, land on the envelope, ropes over either side, attack both sides at once."

"Risky, but might be doable, depends on the gondola design of the enemy ship."

"Gondola?" Llathia wrinkled her forehead.

"The ship part. If you could get on top of the gondola, there will likely be a hatch that could be forced open.

"What is your best guess about this gondola?"

"I expect it will be somewhere between the Ferandican, which was a box and the Anglian where we have compartments."

"We are getting ahead of ourselves here. First the shakedown cruise and we'll know better what the Flying Elephant can do."

They had the same six people on the ship.

"If we cut back on the ballast, we could have more people on board." Llathia eyed the piles of sandbags.

"We could, but it would reduce our vertical maneuverability."

"It would be worth it to be able to board another ship."

"If we can pull it off, yes. Let me think about mechanisms and we can compare ideas." Cal sat on her stool out of the way and got a faraway look in her eyes

"Release ropes," Llathia called out. They'd reduced the ballast by a couple hundred pounds. Easy enough to control with ropes and easier on the sandbags.

Kkitatin waved as they rose over the jungle and headed south. Llathia didn't think she'd ever get used to flying high over the canopy. Birds were specks below them.

"Set engines to half ahead. We are going to the next mountain, around it and back. Stay alert."

The sun was warm. Cal said the air got cold high above. They'd have to think about warm clothes. Not a common item in equatorial Harasah, but doable. Anything was doable.

With little wind, llathia allowed herself to enjoy the flight. Halfway to their goal, they dropped some ballast pouring the sand out of the bags since they had time.

The jungle became green fuzz below them and the air made her shiver.

"Hold at this height." They were now higher than the eagles flew.

The mountain came closer.

"Ahead two-thirds," Llathia ordered. The engines chugged faster.

She estimated they were another hour from the near side of the mountain, but they hadn't tested the props above two-thirds.

Something above her snapped and the ship tilted to the port side.

"Hold tight, douse the fires. Stand on the upper side." Llathia spilled some air from the balloons, and they started to drop. She looked for a clearing to land in, but from this height it was hard.

The jungle grew closer, but there was no safe place to land.

Then another snap and they tilted 30 degrees to port. Sandbags rolled across the floor and piled up against the port side wall.

"Hold tight, I'm dropping her on the canopy." The port wall split, and they lost their ballast. The Flying Elephant soared higher. "Blast it. Roll call."

"Cal here."

"Hovid here."

"Monsha here."

No other voices called and llathia wanted to swear.

"Spilling more air. It is going to be a rough landing. Don't let yourself slide, tie in if you have to, we may stop still high up."

They dropped and the balloons flapped above them.

The Flying Elephant hit the canopy and crunched. The balloons collapsed on top of them. The left boiler and engine fell from the ship, but this time the Flying Elephant didn't soar back into the air. The gondola jerked to a stop and llathia still couldn't see the ground.

"I'm going to climb down the tether rope," Cal said. "I'll shout when I see the ground."

"Why you?"

"I trained for it." Cal climbed out the starboard window. "I'll need a hand to get to the rope."

Hovid and Monsha held Cal's left arm, she got her legs on the rope and found a handhold.

"Release."

The woman slid down the rope faster than llathia had expected.

"You're about fifty feet up." She shouted from below. "Wrap the rope around your bottom foot and use that to control your speed. Too slow is better than too fast."

Llathia let Hovid and Monsha lower her out the window. She caught the rope with her feet like Cal had and slowly slid down the rope.

"I'm at the bottom," Llathia called up and went to stand beside Cal. Hovid followed, then Monsha.

"Cave is that way." Monsha pointed.

"Mark it on the ground. We need to assess the situation before we start walking." Cal said. "Any injuries you haven't noticed? Even something minor could become a problem."

"I'm good," Llathia said. She wanted to resent Cal for taking control, but she'd just crashed her ship. She didn't deserve command.

"I'm fine," Monsha reported.

"I've got a long scrape on my left leg. It isn't bleeding but is oozing blood." Hovid sounded surprised.

"Anyone have a knife?" Cal asked.

Llathia shook her head. Another thing to add to the list of her failures.

Cal accepted a knife from Monsha. "Back in a bit. Hang tight." She went up the rope. Llathia waited with her heart in her throat until Cal reappeared with a roughly cut sheet of fabric.

"Let me bandage Hovid's leg." She cut the fabric into strips, then handed the knife back to Monsha. Cal bandaged the leg efficiently. "Right, let's go. Monsha, you have the lead, I'll take the rear.

"If at any moment you think you are lost. Stop and shout for help." Monsha waved at the jungle. "You can get lost in just a few steps. Don't let feeling foolish kill you."

"I'm sorry," Llathia blurted out the words.

"We should be thanking you," Cal said. "The ship had a catastrophic failure, but you somehow got us on the ground. There is always a risk. You acted when you needed to."

Hovid and Monsha nodded; llathia's legs gave out and she sobbed. Two people were dead, and despite Cal's words, she felt the burden of those deaths on her soul. Cal knelt beside her and wrapped an arm around her shoulders.

"Let it out. Then we'll get started."

***

Roger looked again for the Flying Elephant. They were long overdue.

"What if they crashed?" kkitatin's lips trembled. "What if they are all dead?"

"There are a lot of things that might have happened. We can't assume they're dead." Roger wished he believed his own words. "In the morning I'll send some warriors to search for them. The mountain they were aiming for is three days walk through the jungle. We'll find them."

Roger wanted to go himself, but he didn't know the jungle in this area. He would be in the way.

Voz'ci put a hand on Roger's shoulder. Roger took his daughter's hand and led the way to the village.

CHAPTER 16 CAT AND MOUSE

Bri Curzem looked out at the rain pouring down on the Capital. It was a perfect day to go out.

"I'm taking a coach to the exhibition."

"You should stay here." Sigrid stared at him coldly. "The exhibition has nothing to do with you."

"Very well." Bri shrugged maybe a bit too theatrically, but she didn't react to it. "You can entertain the duchess when she drops in for tea. The woman is insufferably nosy. I will be in my bed with a fever, which will be the only excuse she might accept."

"She won't be allowed in." Sigrid made a slashing motion with her hand.

"Then the Kershian Embassy will become the gossip of the city. We won't be able to make a move without people talking about it. It wouldn't be a problem for me, but the rumour mill is already talking about the return of the woman who broke up the scandalous relationship of the decade."

"Very well. You will take a guard with you."

"He can wait in the coach. An armed and uniformed Kershian will not be welcome."

Sigrid stared at him again, then waved her hand in dismissal.

He'd never liked the woman, but outside of her expertise, she was surprisingly easy to manipulate. Bri found his favourite guard, a lazy and drunken man who would sleep away the day and give Bri a head start. Then it would be a contest between his local connections and Sigrid's single-mindedness.

Calliope and the Engine Smith

The exhibition was everything it had been advertised, a potpourri of up-and-coming artists. The variety was extraordinary. Kershian art reflected the moods and tastes of the emperor, since he was always grouchy and had no taste, it tended toward the martial and patriotic. Bri walked about chatting with the others viewing the show, then when the rain thickened to a grey sheet. He strolled out the front door and down the street. It would be a long walk in the rain to his contact on the seedier side of town, but he relished the freedom.

Sigrid hadn't said anything, but Bri's contacts had told the story of the school fire. Reading between the lines, he had to assume she'd made it free. Logically Sigrid would be sent out to make Astrid vanish, so showing up here strongly suggested she expected Astrid to arrive in Anglia.

He had to find her first, then guard against the shadows. It had been a long time since his active days as an agent. Hopefully, he hadn't forgotten too much.

***

"Except for the language, we might as well be back at school in Mzorat." Astrid flopped on her bed.

"Well, the staff is politer," Gretta said from her side of the room.

"There is that." Astrid sat up. "I'm feeling just as trapped."

"Understandable, but going outside would be the height of foolishness."

"I yearn for the days when I could be as foolish as I pleased and only risk a beating."

"Good evening, my ladies." Their 'maid' knocked and came into the room. "Lights out is in twenty minutes."

"Thanks, Fran." Astrid studied the maid. She looked the part, but they'd been told she was a special agent. "Hypothetically speaking, would it be possible to get a message to Commander McAllen?"

"And why would you be wishing to send a message to Mr. McAllen?" Fran picked up the dresses they'd worn that day. Somehow the trunks had held a few clothes that fit Astrid and Gretta and each time Fran picked up laundry, she replaced the ones that didn't fit.

"I'm worried about my father."

"That's a dangerous thing." Fran straightened the clothes in their wardrobes. "Knowledge leads to action. Action is risky."

"I know," Astrid said, "but he's the only family I have left, aside from Gretta."

"I believe you have a test tomorrow. A good night's sleep will help you do well."

Fran closed the door and left them alone.

"Was that a yes or no?" Astrid asked.

"That was 'it goes over my head'." Gretta lay down. "I'm going to sleep. I suggest you try as well."

***

Fran sighed and headed for the Principal's office. She knocked and entered.

"Pardon the intrusion, ma'am, but I'm concerned that keeping Astrid in the dark will lead to her attempting something foolish. She did after all escape that school in Mzorat and allegedly burned it down."

"What do you suggest?"

"Perhaps a visit from her Uncle John will ease her concerns."

"Or heighten them and increase the likelihood of her jumping the wall."

"I think she is wise enough not to leap into action without careful thought."

"Do we have any word on the father?"

"Our best guess is he's gone into hiding. The activity of the Kershian agents has increased, but more like they are looking for someone than gathering information."

"They could be looking for our Astrid."

"The areas they are searching are neighbourhoods that would pose as much danger to her as letting her go on her own, probably more."

"Very well." The principal turned back to her paperwork. "I will arrange a letter from Uncle John."

***

Bri lay low behind a pile of trash. He was going to have to find a different hideout. The agents were getting too close for comfort. Back down the alley, it looked like a dead end, but Bri climbed the oddly sturdy drainpipe to the roof, then scuttled away. He could make a block before he had to come down to the street.

"Ain't you the athletic one." A dark-haired prostitute put her hand on his arm. She had to be desperate if she was propositioning Bri the way he was dressed now.

"Sorry, lovey, not tonight."

"Them folks is looking for you." She peered at him. "Look past the grime and you're the fellow, sure as sure."

"Very well, then." Bri offered his arm.

"A gentlemen. What's to stop me calling out now?"

"They'd kill you and leave it to look like we did each other in. I, on the other hand, can't afford to leave a trail."

"Cost you a hundred guineas."

"Deal," Bri responded without hesitation. He slipped a purse into her hand. "I give you the other half when we get to where you live."

"Where I live?" She looked at him with fear in her eyes.

"I'm not one for rutting in the streets."

She led him down the street, and Bri felt eyes on him. *Let them be searching, not hunting.*

Up rickety stairs and down a reeking, dingy hall, she came to a door.

"Got to make sure the place is empty." She knocked on the door and waited. "No one home." She pushed the door open. "Go on in."

"Ladies first." Bri shoved her through the door and followed close on her heels.

The bruiser had to be the biggest man Bri had ever seen. The hooker tried to dodge to the side, but Bri shoved her into the brute and scanned the room. No other surprises. The big man slapped the woman to one side and charged Bri with the monstrous butcher's knife.

Bri sidestepped the jab with the knife and punched the man in the throat, then slipped behind the man, kicked his knee and broke his neck as the man crashed to the floor. He caught the knife before it hit the floor and held it to the woman's throat.

"I don't particularly want to kill you, but I will if you force me," Bri said in a conversational tone. "You should think more about why someone is being looked for." He took the purse from her hand and stuck it in her mouth, then used the knife to cut the sleeve of the woman's dress off. He gagged her, then tied her hands.

Sounds of the hallway creaking alerted him. *Damn, they were fast.* He pushed the brute against the door, then dragged the woman into the other room.

Sigrid stood with a knife against a little girl's neck.

"You've got soft…

Bri threw the knife hoping to distract the killer and let him get close enough to go hand to hand. It cut the girl's ribcage and stuck into Sigrid's side. The little girl slumped to the floor as Sigrid snarled, yanking the knife out of her ribs and throwing it at him. Bri sidestepped and crouched, hands up. He'd never liked knives much, they left too much mess.

They circled, Sigrid feinting with her blade, but Bri didn't buy it. She was buying time. Someone was attacking the door.

Sigrid lunged, for real this time, Bri barely escaped with a slash on his arm. He headbutted Sigrid and grabbed her knife hand.

"You're dead, then your girl." Sigrid kneed him and twisted away, then stopped and stared down at her chest where the point of the butcher knife stuck out of her chest. Unbelievably, Sigrid turned to slash at the prostitute's face.

Bri jumped forward and kicked Sigrid against the wall, took her knife and stabbed it through the back of her skull.

"Your girl isn't dead, get her to a doctor, then leave town and never come back."

She snatched up the child and vanished behind a blanket hanging on the back of the room.

"You're good as dead, traitor." A voice shouted through the door and kept kicking it. "I'll come in and watch her slice you up into fine little pieces."

Bri searched Sigrid and came up with a revolver. As the door splintered, he fired through the hole, someone grunted on the other side and another voice swore. Bri emptied the gun through the wall. Another person screamed on the far side as Bri followed the woman and child through the hole in the wall. He wound at random through halls and rooms avoiding anywhere he heard noises.

He came out into the filthiest alley he'd ever encountered.

If Sigrid was looking for Astrid, then he needed to create a diversion for her. Get the emperor's anger pointed in a different direction.

Step one was to get off Anglia, then he could appear on the continent and cause trouble. His arm would hold for a bit. He headed toward where he'd been holing up to pick up a few things, then he'd disappear from Anglia for good.

Astrid was probably safer here than anywhere else in the world.

Chapter 17 Spreading Wings

The second day after the crash, Cal followed behind llathia, worrying at the woman's lack of confidence. Cal didn't think she could have done any better herself. It would have to work itself out. Llathia was very conscious of her position. Though she'd relaxed considerably in the last week or two, she was still Lady Mtuaka with all the responsibilities to go with it. For all Cal's fancy titles, she'd never had responsibility for ordinary civilians.

Monsha stopped suddenly and put his hands up. Three men stood blocking the path.

"We are heading back to Mtuaka lands."

"Did you fall out of the sky?" one asked in oddly accented Congu.

"Yes." Monsha pointed behind him. "The ship is still there. You can have whatever you want from it."

"What would we do with a sky ship?"

"There is enough cloth to make tents for your whole clan, or you can sell it back to the Mtuaka."

"What would you trade for this cloth? Your coins and gold are useless."

"What do you need?" Monsha spread his arms.

"Axes, hoes, tools of steel that won't break."

"Like this?" Cal pulled the knife/hairpin from her hair and offered it to one.

He examined it curiously.

"It is sharp but too small to be more than a toy." He tossed it on the ground.

"This may be more to your liking." Monsha offered his knife which gained a much higher evaluation.

"The jungle says people are looking for you. We will take you to meet them." They turned and walked in a slightly different direction than Monsha was leading them. Cal picked up the tiny knife and put it back in her hair.

"What does the white one want with the toy?" The speaker turned to frown at Cal.

"It is small, like jewellery. A woman needs something to know she is safe." The man put his hand out and Cal dropped the knife in it. He said something in a different language, and the other two men laughed. They continued on their way, occasionally saying something to the speaker and laughing, but he laughed as well and didn't look angry.

The men walked at a faster pace than Monsha, though they were smaller in size. Cal had to work hard to keep up. Llathia too looked like she was thinking more about walking than the crash.

"Hurry, it will be dark soon." The speaker picked up the pace. "Your people are close."

An hour later, during that brief moment of twilight before the jungle night fell, when they met three Mtuaka warriors. Monsha went and muttered to them briefly.

"A blade in thanks for guiding our companions, and one for your chieftain." They passed over three knives. The guides took them without thanks, then vanished into the jungle.

"We'll stay here tonight. We'll be safe enough with the people of the jungle in the area." The lead warrior said. "You will be back to the village by nightfall tomorrow." He put fingers in his mouth and gave a piercing whistle, then held up a hand for silence. A faint whistle came back to them.

"You will be hungry." The lead warrior pulled bread and fruit from a bag at his waist. "Eat. We'll eat tomorrow."

***

Three days after they'd returned to the engine smith village, Cal had the framework for a new gondola in place. While she was cutting fabric on the old ship, she'd looked for the failure points. The rope attaching the gondola to the balloon had snapped. It didn't look any different from the others, so Cal wondered if the weight hadn't been distributed evenly.

Llathia had been notable by her absence. 'Taking care of clan business.' She'd said and returned to the staal. Kkitatin and Roger were at Kkittu surveying plans for a new village.

Cal had no idea how to work with the wood boilers and the engines llathia had made. She'd sent a letter to Lusundi to be given to the next southbound Anglian ship months ago along with the order for the boiler and fabric. Cal didn't expect any result from it, but she couldn't let go of the new idea floating in her head.

When the new ship was ready for the engines to be installed, Cal headed for the Mtuaka staal to talk sense into llathia.

At the staal, First Wife shook her head when Cal asked to talk to llathia.

"Pass a message to her for me. 'Did you give up when your father died? We are working with danger greater than lions or river horses, tragedy will happen, but we use it to improve. I can't work with her wood engines, so if she doesn't come and help, I'll have to try using the iron engine from the boats, even if I have to snatch the second one from the jaws of a crocodile.'

She left an open-mouthed First Wife and trekked back to the cave.

"While we're waiting for the engine smith, we are going to build something she designed." Cal held up a model of the eagle. "If you think the Flying Elephant was dangerous, this is like hunting a crocodile with a knife by comparison."

They used the reeds to form the skeleton, but getting enough cloth for the wings was difficult. They stretched the last bit they had over the skeleton, then used the up and down balloon to hoist it and a log up to the top of the cliff. Chiza wasn't there, but the foresters helped her set up the eagle with the log in place.

"I'm going to observe from the balloon. Tie it off to a tree so I don't float away."

When she was ready the foresters carefully threw the eagle off the cliff, it soared fifty feet from the edge before the wings folded and it crashed to the ground.

"We'll need more reeds."

***

Astrid dumped her books on the desk in her room.

"I know that look." Gretta put her own pile down neatly. "You're plotting something."

"I didn't escape Mzorat to idle away my time in Anglia."

"I don't know if a repeat of Mzorat will make us many friends in high places."

"True, and there's nobody here I really want to slap, so we need something other than *les majeste* to get us kicked out."

"You weren't going to be kicked out, they were going to hang you."

"Details." Astrid waved a hand and laughed, then went serious. "There are at least two ways to get in or out of the school."

"Apparently it is marriage or graduation." Gretta held up her hands as Astrid glared at her.

"Another reason to escape. There are some serious matchmakers here and it is getting harder to find reasons why I can't let any offers be sent to my father."

"You could have told them you were betrothed already."

"Then I would have had to come up with endless lies about the poor man. Father always said to keep the story simple."

"What do you think of the message from Uncle John? Speaking of your father."

"Hopeful. If they'd found a body, I hope they would have told me. So he's played some game in the nether regions of the capital then vanished." Astrid flopped on the bed and put her hands behind her head. "Back to escaping, we really have two escapes to plan. The first is getting out of the school, the second will be getting off Anglia."

"Can't we just get a berth on a steamer again?"

"We had the letter from Mr. Strathes, and we were heading toward Anglia. This time we have no letter and we're running away. I don't expect we'd have nearly such a warm welcome a second time."

Gretta put the kettle on the tiny burner they were allowed.

"No, we are not lighting a fire," she wagged a finger at Astrid.

"It would be a poor return for their hospitality, and I don't expect it would work. No, we go out the front gate with a pass, or we leave through whatever tunnel the visitors use."

"I don't think a pass will work, even the senior students don't go out without guards following them."

"Probably this place is part of the training program for covert operations. 'Follow this student and don't get busted or you fail and go back to swabbing decks.'" Astrid deepened her voice and made a stern face. Gretta laughed.

"All the more reason not to go out the front gate."

"That leaves the not-so-secret passage." Astrid sat up. "Have you noticed that all the special visits happen in the Principal's office?"

"It makes sense since she'd have to arrange them."

"And because the passage comes out in her office."

"How do figure that?"

Astrid lifted a finger. "Her office is the last door in the hallway and there are windows overlooking the campus to the west and the north.

"That's a good reason it doesn't come out in her office." Gretta shook her head and poured water into the teapot to warm it up.

"True, if the passage was against the outside wall, but I suspect it is between the Principal's office and the secretary's next door. The way the secretary's office is laid out, you can't see to the back of it."

"Student records are in there."

"True, but why have the adjoining door between the offices come out in the confidential records section?"

"Maybe so the Principal can look up records herself."

"Why have a secretary at all if she's going to manage everything herself?"

"But the Principal's office? Why make it so obvious?" Gretta added tea leaves and poured water into the pot.

"Because it is obvious, but also a special visitor risks being spotted, even at night, and the rumour mill has never mentioned that happening."

"We break into the Principal's office, open the door to a secret entrance, then come out where?"

"Probably the Admiralty somewhere." Astrid lay down and stared at the ceiling. "The thing with the Admiralty is it's a big place, and not everyone there will know who we are. Commander McAllen, Uncle John, the Queen, who else would know?"

"How will that help us?"

"Once we get to the Admiralty, we let them escort us out of there and we vanish."

"That sounds as likely as stealing the emperor's black coach to make our escape."

"At least if we fail, we deal with some embarrassment, not a one-way ride."

Gretta added the cream and sugar and handed a cup to Astrid.

"The biggest challenge will be hiding out until we can reasonably be caught at the admiralty."

"I do have to admit that the life here is dull compared to running for our lives constantly. There are pilgrims who make the round of the older church, everyone from wealthy to the poor who work their way in hostels along the path. Once we get to the continent, we can be pilgrims."

"How do you know so much about this?"

"Reading." Gretta turned pink. "I was looking up a bit about Svan's family. They manage all the hostels across Kershia."

"We wear our oldest dresses and take only what we can hide on our persons."

"I'm guessing you want to try tonight?"

"I'm getting antsy doing nothing. Saving the empire will involve much higher risks than escaping school."

Gretta sipped at her tea and rolled her eyes. "We'd be better to raid the prop room for the theatre, it doesn't ever seem to be locked."

"Brilliant idea."

***

Talking about sneaking out in the early morning was easy, carrying it off would take a great deal of luck and what the seniors at Mzorat called 'brass'.

Gretta volunteered to raid the prop room, while Astrid ran through scenarios in her head. They arranged to get up in the early morning by the simple expedient of drinking a pot of tea each.

"Put a middling dress on over the rags," Astrid ordered.

They visited the washroom and Astrid led the way through the building. "Wait here." Astrid flattened herself again a door. A woman walked past carrying a tiny lamp. "Next best thing to a wall of thorns between the boys' dorm and the girls'," Astrid whispered when the woman was out of sight. "This way."

"How long have you been scouting this?" Gretta whispered.

"I've been having trouble sleeping at night." Astrid took Gretta's hand and led her down the hallway to the door between the student dorms and the staff residences.

"The younger teachers make extra doing these nighttime walks." Astrid took the first staircase down to the main level where the offices were. She knelt beside the principal's door and used a hat pin to feel around in the lock. It snicked open and Astrid heaved a sigh. "I wasn't sure the principal's would be the same lock."

The office was only lit by a bit of light from the windows. The carpets muffled their footsteps as they tiptoed to the door that, according to Astrid, led to a secret passage. The door opened and they slipped through, closing it behind them and leaving them in pitch dark. Astrid lit a match and put it to the candle she'd brought. They were in a tiny room with no other exit. The only feature was a level pointing up. Astrid pushed it down and the floor started dropping beneath them it stopped where a grate separated them from a dark expanse. It pushed easily to the side, and they stepped out onto a platform. A cylindrical tunnel led away. Astrid jumped down then helped Gretta.

"I didn't expect a train tunnel."

They walked into the tunnel hand in hand. Every hundred or so steps there was a little alcove. They'd been walking for what felt like hours when a breeze blew out their candle.

"Quick." Astrid pulled Gretta along and into one of the alcoves. Nothing happened for so long that Astrid wondered if she'd made a mistake, but then a train that filled the tunnel trundled past. She didn't recognize the man on the train, but from his uniform he was important. As soon as the coach passed, they ran down the tunnel to the faint light in the distance.

Astrid boosted Gretta to the platform, then clambered up.

"No soot." She looked at her hands. "Strange." They walked along to another grate. They pushed it aside and stepped in. Astrid pushed the lever up, but nothing happened.

"Close the grate," Gretta suggested. This time the floor lifted them up and stopped in by a door. Astrid put an ear to the door and heard nothing. She pushed on the door, then slipped out into the room.

It didn't look like the room at the end of a secret passage, but Astrid heaved a sigh of relief, it was empty. She tried the door, and it wasn't locked, but after they'd stepped through it locked behind them.

She lit the candle again. The hall had marble floors and paintings of ships hung on the walls. Some of them showed sea battles. The doors along the hall had gilded knobs. They crept along the hall to the door at the end and opened it a crack, the faintest grey came through.

"I don't hear anything," Astrid whispered and pushed the door the rest of the way open.

"Hoy, where did you come from?" The man in uniform had a stern look on what might have otherwise been a friendly face.

"Oh, it's been terrible. We went in to find my boyfriend, he works in some office, then all the lights went out and..." Gretta wailed

"And I suggested we try to find our way out before the people start arriving." Astrid rolled her eyes. "Sella's afraid of the dark, poor soul."

"Well, you come with me." The man led them along a short hall, then opened a door and waved them in. Grey light came in a window illuminating a wooden table and chairs. The door closed behind them with a snap. There was no knob on the inside.

"We may as well sit down." Astrid slumped into a chair. "I'm guessing he didn't buy our story of visiting a boyfriend."

"It was all I could think of," Gretta said. "Sorry."

"Don't be sorry, it is more than I came up with."

By the light filtering down through the barred window, it was full morning when the door opened behind them.

"You certainly know how to create a fuss."

Astrid looked up. "Fran?"

"Do you know how many alarms you two set off?"

"Alarms?" Gretta frowned. "I didn't hear anything."

"You wouldn't have." Fran crossed her arms and glared at them. "What am I going to do with you?"

"You will let us go." Astrid stood. "I appreciate the hospitality, but I have work to do. Unless Anglia is willing to hold an imperial heir in prison, I will be leaving."

"Let me get you out of here, then we'll talk." Fran knocked on the door. It opened to show the stern navy man. "I will take it from here." Fran walked out and looked back. "Move it you two, I expect a full report on this fiasco before breakfast. My apologies, ensign, a training exercise got a little out of control." Her ice-cold voice had Astrid's gut in a knot. Fran escorted them out of the building. Her uniform obviously showed she was important, and no one questioned them, though there were plenty of covert stares.

Outside a coach waited for them. Fran waved them in.

"Once we figured out what was going on, we realized you were serious about leaving. We have no right to hold you but didn't expect you to use a classified national secret to make your escape." Fran snorted. "You could have come up with that speech and we'd have let you walk out."

"Walk out and be spotted by how many eyes?" Astrid said. "This has been about avoiding my own people, not yours."

"What was your plan from here?"

"Pilgrimage, it was Gretta's idea. There are any number of pilgrims on tour."

"A good thought, but you should have an adult to avoid questions. Two young girls heading out on their own is begging for trouble." Fran shook her head. "I'll come along, they won't be looking for a family of three and her Majesty would be displeased if you were caught or killed."

***

Llathia screamed in rage and stormed through her rooms. She hadn't been so angry since N'toox attacked her. Cal's message as much as called her a coward. What made her most angry was she agreed.

"What am I going to do?" she roared at Chiza.

"Either you go, or you stay." He crossed his arms.

"That's no help."

"Prince Roger is asking for help building a defence at Kkittu, he doesn't like having an open landing for the Kershians."

"I will go and have a look." Llathia went to take a bath, then dressed with extra attention to Thasi's prompting.

"Let's go, Chiza."

Roger's warriors had cleared away the rubble by tossing the burnt wood in the river and setting the stone aside to be reused.

"Why now?" Llathia demanded.

"Kkitatin wanted to rebuild. This is at least a beginning."

"You do everything kkitatin says?"

"I do when she's right." Roger met her gaze. "Do I get your help or not?"

"I will arrange for trees to be brought; you can use them as you will."

"Thank you, Lady Mtuaka." Roger bowed, Anglian style. Llathia wanted to slap him, but it wouldn't be smart to irritate the king.

Back at the staal, a woman came up to her. "Some of the jungle-born are here with more cloth than I know what to do with, and they want iron tools in exchange."

"Give them whatever they want, then load the cloth on a wagon. I have a ship to build."

***

While waiting for the next lot of giant reeds, Cal realized that none of the Congu knew how to run the iron steam engine. They pulled the parts from the wagon, and she made them assemble it, test it, take it apart and assemble it again until it met her exacting standard.

"You need to pay attention to the dials." She tapped them. "They will tell you when to pump in water and when to build the fire up. If you are going to capture a Kershian ship, you'll need to know how to fly it."

Since they didn't have a ship to put it in, Cal had them find a wagon and turn it into a steam coach. This one went faster than a crawl, but it was dangerous on anything like rough ground.

A wagon arrived with Commander McAllen riding beside the Congu driver.

"Himself told me to find out what you were up to with top-secret mechanics."

"I hope, building something faster than an air ship, but more likely, getting myself killed."

"Sounds like fun." McAllen patted the wagon. "Everything you asked for is here, but it took a direct order from the queen to release it."

"Did you find the traitor?"

"An anonymous letter suggested we investigate someone. From there it was easy enough."

"Convenient." Cal twisted her mouth.

"You're telling me. By the way, your Kershian princess jumped the wall with her friend and one of our better agents in tow. She'll be raising hell in Kershia soon enough."

"I don't think it will be soon enough. The Kershians will invade, our lives and Astrid's depend on how we meet them."

"Latest intelligence suggests no more than six weeks. The emperor is eager to launch his attack. He's even talking about coming in person to direct the battle."

"We can always hope." Cal laughed. "That could take care of our problem and Astrid's at the same time.

"General Mizvrat will find a way to restrain him."

"Time to get to work then."

Llathia showed up with a face like a thundercloud and Chiza looking stolid behind her. On the wagon was a huge pile of fabric.

"I got your message."

"I'm glad," Cal said. "I can't do this without you."

***

That wasn't what llathia expected to hear. Disdain, anger, pity – not this simple welcome.

"Then let's get to work." Llathia walked past then stopped at the pile of twisted reeds.

"What is that?"

"We tried building your eagle, but it failed. We're waiting for more reeds." Cal took her through the clearing and explaining what had been done.

"We have two bottle trees, we can use them to make the boiler, what about using the iron engine?"

"Possible, if we can balance the weight properly."

"What if you had the other one from the river?"

"That would make it easier."

"I need to borrow your steam coach. Prince Roger asked for some help building defences at Kkittu. I'll get my warriors to fetch your second engine and boiler."

"I will go and help them," Hovid said. "They need me to drive the coach."

"Thank you, Hovid." Something lifted off llathia's shoulder. No one blamed her, only she had taken on fault for the crash.

"Let's get to work," Cal said. "We're on the clock. Maybe six weeks, but I want to be ready in position in four. It won't do any good to arrive late to the party."

A team of people from the village attacked the balloon fabric, repairing tears and inspecting every finger's breadth.

Another Anglian had arrived with a wagon load of things.

"Can't wait to see what you do with this stuff," he said and left the wagon in the village. "But duty calls. Himself says hello."

Chapter 18 The Eagle

The reeds arrived and Cal worked on the new Eagle. She studied each place where the first one had bent, folded or broken and using triangles to make it stronger, but not much heavier. Llathia was checking the work on the balloon. In a few places, she insisted on patches over the damage. Her funk, or whatever it was had vanished.

Cal bent reeds the thickness of her thumb to make the top of the wing curved like an eagle's. The research llathia had done was impressive but Cal worried that they were arriving at the limit of what could be done with reeds and fabric. At least they had plenty of fabric now.

"Llathia, I'm ready for a drop test. You want to supervise?"

"Coming." She trotted over and checked the ropes fastening the eagle to the up and down balloon, then climbed into the basket.

Cal waited back at the edge of the jungle where she could barely just see the top of the cliff without a crick in her neck. The balloon arrived and specks moved. It had to have been an hour later when the Eagle soared away from the cliff. It circled slowly down. The others stopped work to watch it float until it settled in the clearing.

Llathia had followed it down with the balloon.

"Amazing!" Her face glowed with excitement as she landed the balloon and made it fast before running over to examine the Eagle. "I don't see any stress points, no breaks. I'm going to take it up again."

The rest of the day was spent watching the Eagle glide down in circles and checking for damage. As night approached, they moved the glider into the cave and headed for the village.

"Tomorrow I'm flying it," Llathia said.

"That is the next step," Cal said reluctantly. "Are you sure you want to risk it yourself?"

"I have to. I can't ask someone else to do what's never been done before."

"One more test, I have an idea about steering. I'll build a small version to test it."

"I will fly tomorrow, but I'd like to see your steering mechanism." Llathia was practically bouncing on her toes.

"I think moving the body weight forward or back, and maybe side to side."

"Good thinking, we'd need two slings to hold the weight of the body and let the arms move you." Llathia turned around.

"Tomorrow," Cal laughed and grabbed llathia's hand. "I will help you build it."

***

Llathia's stomach was in knots.

"When you stepped into the arena against N'toox, everyone thought you'd die."

"Except me."

"Except you." Chiza hugged her tightly. "Believe in yourself."

"Cal said she's alive because she never completely trusts her work."

"Trust yourself." He stepped back. "If anyone can do this, it will be you."

They arrived at the clearing to find Cal already at work on the eagle.

"Lie down see if your weight is distributed right." She pointed to the sling. "Left your legs free for the landing. You can pull them up when you're flying.

Llathia experimented with it awkwardly.

"I'm ready." Llathia stood up. "It's time." She kissed and Chiza. "I love you."

They fastened the Eagle to the balloon, then llathia watched the ground shrink below her. She landed the glider, then waited for it to be untied before she brought the balloon to rest.

"Last check." Llathia made herself go over the Eagle as she had so many times the day before. She picked up the glider, amazed again at how little it weighed. Then without warning, she ran and jumped off the edge of the cliff.

The nose of the Eagle raised up. Llathia pulled herself forward on the sling, now the nose went down, but it didn't fall. She stared down at the ground turning below her, tried to lean out of the spin and the glide straightened.

She was flying. Soaring in the eagle's space. The birds had moved away from the cliff with all the activity, but she thanked them with a whisper. Gradually llathia experimented with larger movements and was able to turn the Eagle in either direction and control the speed of her forward motion. It wouldn't let her gain height. After two heart-stopping attempts that convinced her she was going to die, llathia contented herself with a slow circle down.

How am I going to land? She made plans as the ground seemed to rush at her. How did the eagles land? Wings wide, legs outstretched, then folding their wings. She couldn't fold her wings, but she could do the rest.

The ground blurred past, she was below the treetops now and had to turn tightly. In the end, she had no time to plan. Throwing her legs forward, her toes brushed the ground. Then nose went up and dropped the Eagle on the ground. Her heart pounded painfully, but she couldn't stop grinning.

Everyone around burst into mad cheers. Chiza swept her up as they lifted the Eagle away from her.

"I want to say never do that again, but I know you will. Build me one and let us fly together."

She flew twice more that day before Cal pointed at a place on the frame that was splitting.

"We'll have it fixed for tomorrow."

"Tomorrow we'll build more. If we get above another airship, we can use the Eagle to board it."

Cal laughed. "Right you are then."

***

The next week they made four more Eagles. Each one was tested with a log. Monsha complained that he didn't want to wait, but when his glider folded and plummeted, spinning to the ground, he admitted it was a good idea.

Cal tried it but decided she preferred the solidity of an airship around her.

Hovid returned with another boiler and engine. They spent two days cleaning the mud away and checking the pieces.

"Might as well put it together on the new airship."

"Let's call this one the Lion," Llathia suggested.

The Lion passed its tests as if it was as eager to fly as the people building it. They built two disc throwers on each side and put the ballast behind a net. They made the ropes holding the gondola a web so a failure wouldn't throw the ship off balance. Instead of throwing them out a window, they cut a hole in the floor just big enough for the sand to drop through.

"What are you going to use those things your friend left here?" Llathia asked as they walked to the cave one morning.

"I have an idea, but it is crazy. I mean even crazier than the eagle."

"Now you have to tell me."

"We have weapons to use against other airships, and we can drop sandbags on ground troops, but how do we destroy a navy vessel?"

"So?"

"A steam canon. Remember I was experimenting with them earlier. We fire things like oversized spears down, even straight down, that won't take as much pressure and we have the pipes McAllen brought, and the steam ball to power it. I'll have to create a way to load it and keep the spear from falling out before we shoot."

"Why is it crazy?"

"Last time I built one, it worked but destroyed the ship I was on."

"An air ship?"

"No," Cal shook her head at the memory. "A derelict naval ship."

"Well, at least you know it can wreck a navy ship."

"We need to fire it more than once."

***

The cannons weren't as hard to put together as Cal had feared. They weren't accurate at any horizontal distance, but Cal hoped firing down would be better.

"We have a problem." Roger showed up as they put the finishing touches on the pivots and braces for the cannon.

"Word from the other side of the river is the Kershians are ramping up for a second invasion. Fresh troops are arriving, and they've built more boats."

"Great, we need a chance to test the Lion," Llathia said, suddenly sounding like Lady Mtuaka. "I will put two hundred warriors under your command.

We'll draw them in, then destroy them." Roger promised.

"They have to make it to shore." Lady Mtuaka said. "I don't intend to let that happen."

***

"Svan's parents are not happy with the invasion of Harasah, not because of the ethics of the action, but because Svan will be on one of the ships," Astrid said. "A lot of the lesser families are in the same situation. They haven't tapped into the money being made by the war effort, but they look to lose members of their families, and their taxes have gone up."

"The lesser families will likely support us, but they have a minority of votes in the council." Gretta stretched. "We need at least two of the five major houses and a majority of the lesser houses, and that is only to bring the charges."

"If the invasion is successful, you would be best to vanish." Fran poured tea for them in the small hostel where they were staying. The rural countryside looked peaceful. Here it was smaller farms, the acres of vineyards were closer to the sea."

"If only there was a safe place to vanish." Astrid sipped at the hot, bitter liquid and stopped the face she wanted to make. They were dirt-poor Anglian pilgrims doing the round of ancient churches, cream and sugar wasn't on the menu.

"A disastrous campaign will give you a chance, but I wouldn't put it at even odds." Fran shrugged.

"I went into this knowing the odds." Astrid put the tea aside. "Sowing rumours is slower going than I expected."

"It has its own risks." Fran sipped at her cup and sighed. "What I wouldn't give for hot scones and some butter."

All three of them laughed.

"You keep saying you came to keep us out of trouble." Astrid leaned forward. "I let you come because we wouldn't have escaped without you, but I need to know you aren't spying against Kershia."

"Let me put it this way." Fran put a hand on Astrid's knee. "My mission is not to spy on Kershia, but to help you radically overturn it through an improbable process against impossible odds."

"That makes it sound *so* much better." Gretta giggled.

"Because I'm going against the emperor doesn't mean I'm betraying Kershia."

***

"I'm not betraying Kershia." The chubby vintner looked at Bri like he was a snake in the garden.

"No one's asking you to." Bri gritted his teeth. "Though Kershia, or at least the Emperor, is betraying you. It would be more destructive to your comfortable life for your tax avoidance antics to come out, than for you to support a review of the emperor."

"Angering the emperor would mean the end of our family."

"Do you know that retribution against those who bring a case for a review is illegal?"

"You keep telling me, but the emperor won't care, will he?"

Bri smiled and sipped at his wine. "And that's the whole problem in a nutshell, isn't it?"

Chapter 19 The Battle of Kkittu

They put the Lion on standby, balloon inflated, boilers hot. The Mtuaka warriors set up a relay line through the jungle to the cave to send the whistle down the line. While they waited, Cal played with ways of attaching the Eagles to the Lion's gondola. She'd just settled on hanging them nose down, two on each side when the whistle came. Llathia had insisted on full emergency kits on the ship, axes, knives, rope and more.

"Stations!" Llathia ordered and the crew of the Lion boarded. The eagle flyers came since the Eagles were still fastened.

"It will give us a chance to train." Monsha insisted. Cal took position by the steam cannons, each already loaded with a wad of cloth to hold the spear in place.

"Engineering."

"Go."

"Cannons."

"Go."

"Release ropes."

The Lion leapt into the air as if it was eager for battle. Llathia had the engines turning over just enough to keep them from hitting the cliff face, once they lifted above the cliff, she ordered the engines half ahead and they headed for the river. The warrior watched through the ballast holes in the floor. The muddy silver line of the river came into view.

"Starboard engine one quarter ahead."

The Lion turned to follow the Sombu down to Kkittu.

"Sombi camp on the north bank," Monsha reported

"Monsha, take a flyer down and alert them. We don't want any escaping on the north shore. Take the train if you can; disable it, wreck it, just don't let it get away east."

"Yes, my Lady." Monsha and another warrior climbed out the window and when they were in place the ropes holding were cut and they dropped away.

"Cal watch the Eagles and report." Llathia was feeling the same calmness she had in the arena. Life and death were equally possible, she left all concern behind and concentrated on the battle.

"Aye ma'am," Cal called back. "Both flyers have caught air and are circling down toward the north."

"I see the boats," Hovid shouted. "About a third of the way across the river. Six of them."

"Hold position until they're committed."

"Engine Smith," Cal called.

"Yes."

"Recommend we circle around to put our shadow downstream of the attackers."

"Good thinking, port engine one quarter ahead," Llathia called out the direction to the engineers.

The Lion made its ponderous way around, passing over the north shore and coming up on the boats from the east.

"Engines one quarter." Llathia went back to look through the ballast holes.

The boats looked like toys on the river. "Can we hit them from this height?"

"Only one way to find out," Cal said.

"Ready ballast and hold."

"Cannon primed and ready."

"Ballast ready."

"Drop."

***

Roger watched from the defensive wall they'd rebuilt behind the burned one as the Lion floated high over the invaders.

"Wait until they get on shore before you fire." Roger said conversationally "They'll expect a repeat of last time. We are going to shock them."

Water exploded beside a boat, and the invaders recoiled, but the flat barge didn't tip enough to be a danger to them. Another explosion and the formation broke up. Four boats kept moving forward, two began turning as if to go back to the north shore.

A boom sounded from above and seconds later the boiler on the rearmost boat blew up in a cloud of steam. The boat disintegrated and the soldiers fell into the river. The second boat in the rear fell in half.

A boat ran up onto the shore.

"Wait for them to get on land, I want those guns."

A second made the shore. The next shuddered as a ballast bag crashed through the centre. It swamped and the soldier jumped out rifles held high over their heads. Water exploded near them as they scrambled for shore. The last boat grounded. The soldiers formed up in a line, but some aimed up at the Lion.

"Volley one, fire," Roger yelled and the neat lines of the Kershians fell apart. "Second volley, fire."

The scene on the beach descended into chaos as Kershians ran for the jungle only to meet a hail of arrows.

Some of them threw down their guns and lay on the ground.

"Don't shoot anyone without a weapon," Roger ordered. "Aim for the fancy uniforms. Fire.

"Surrender!" Roger bellowed in Kershian, "and you will not be harmed."

A fight broke out among the Kershians.

"Hold your fire, see who wins." Some of them on the ground jumped up and ran forward with their hands over their heads. Shots from behind knocked some to the ground.

"Anyone with a weapon dies. Fire at will."

The officers in the back were hard to hit without shooting someone who was trying to surrender. Then a ballast bag hit in the middle of the group. The sand obscured them, and when it cleared they were on their knees. A Kershian soldier snatched up rifles and mowed down the officers, then dropped the weapons.

"Hands in the air. Walk forward away from the rifles. Hold. Drop your ammunition, knives and whatever else you may have."

The Kershians stripped down to pants and shirtsleeves.

"We surrender." One of them walked forward and yelled. "We didn't want to fight for them dogs, but they threatened our families. All we want is to farm in peace."

"Wounded step forward. The rest of you sit on the ground, hands behind your head."

***

"They've surrendered," Cal said. "What orders?"

"We go support the Sombi attacking the train." Llathia ordered the ship turned and they headed north.

"Spot that train and we'll try to get over it."

They spotted the train east of the station, the Sombi in a circle around it, but not getting any closer.

"Looks like they've blocked the tracks but can't get to the train."

"We stop over the train and drop ballast."

When the bags hit, dust and sand blew out the windows of the coaches, then soldiers poured out, staggering away from the track. Most of them had dropped their rifles.

"I'm going to go down and take command," Llathia said. "Head east and scout out that coal mine you talked about. Take whatever action you see fit."

Before Cal could argue, llathia climbed out the window and cut the rope holding the glider.

"East it is. One-half engines. We'll follow the track.

***

Cal was worried. They were getting low on fuel by the time they flew over a ramshackle town with a huge pile of coal too close to the ground for the ballast to have the explosive effect it had had on the train. A dozen Kershians ran out pointing at the airship, one of them obviously yelling orders. They shouldered their rifles aiming at the ship.

"Engines full stop." Cal ran to the steam cannon and cursed. She could just see the feet of the front line. "Engines full ahead." The engines surged, then the propellers came apart.

The volley boomed and Cal expected to be torn apart by the bullets, but none came through the gondola. She had a line on the soldiers but was waiting until the officer came into view. Holding a sword of all things and pointing at the gondola.

She fired the cannon and jumped over to the second one and pressurized it but didn't need it. The officer had vanished but for a hand holding his sword. The remaining soldiers were staring at where the man had been or were running for the jungle.

None of them made it. Spears flew from the foliage and dropped them in their tracks.

"Prepare to land," Cal shouted. "It will be rough."

The airship drifted sideways as Cal spilled air. When they scraped the ground, she opened the valves fully. "Douse the fires, maintain pressure. Stay on the ship."

She jumped from the Lion followed by Hovid who was already yelling in Sombi.

The attack group from the jungle had slaughtered all the Kershians, picked up the rifles and were pointing them at Cal and Hovid.

"Hands up, on your knees." She dropped to the ground.

One of the Sombi came over and talked with Hovid. He yelled something and the other Sombi lowered the rifles.

"Since we attacked the Kershians, he's believing us about who we are. They are going to free the rest of their people and respectfully ordered us to stay here." Hovid put his hands down and sprawled on the ground. "Might as well relax."

"Can't relax too much, we need to rebuild the propellers." She went to inspect them. The damage wasn't as bad as she'd feared; they'd be able to limp home with some jury-rigged repairs. "Get on your feet, Monsha; might as work while we wait."

Chapter 20 Aftermath

"You attacked Congu and destroyed a village." Roger kept his face like stone. "Don't tell me we need to tell you we are retaliating. Or are the rules different for Harasah than Loccosia?"

"You're just…" the Kershian officer sneered, then stopped as if only then remembering he was a prisoner.

"Just what?" Roger waited two breaths. "You will strip, and my men will examine your uniforms for anything that could be used as a weapon. Once they are cleared, they will be returned and you will be imprisoned until we have settled an exchange of prisoners."

"You can't hold us, we're—" The officer's words were cut off by a fist to the gut from another man.

"Strip, do not try to hide any weapons. We will remain prisoners until this war is over." The other man looked at the half-dozen officers. "I may not have the highest army rank, but I am first cousin to the Emperor, and as such I'm taking command."

"You can't do that; we won't negotiate with these savages." The officer shouted.

"Strip him and gag him. He can court martial me when I get home." He raised his voice loud enough to be heard by the other group of Kershians. "If they were savages, we'd be dead. Instead, we have been treated with dignity and respect. Remember, we surrendered, under the army code we must be model prisoners as long as we aren't mistreated."

He stripped off his clothes and handed them to a Sombi warrior, who rifled through the pockets and handed them back. He dressed again and laughed. "Look they even left me my cigarettes."

"When they're done, lock them up in decent quarters. We are defending our countries and clans, not making enemies of Kershia." Roger walked over to where Lady Mtuaka spoke with the larger group of prisoners with Chiza looming behind her.

"You will be transported across the river where you will work in the rebuilding of the village you destroyed. If you don't wish to work, you may be imprisoned with the officers."

"I got nothing against honest work." A big man stood up. "I am Heod, the leader of the Kershians who grew up in this land. We wanted nothing of this war, we just want to go home."

"King vvatha has already declared that you may stay and keep your holdings subject to a tax to the king." Lady Mtuaka stated

"That's not what we were told. They said that was lies to keep us quiet."

"Did anyone come to drive you from your home?"

"No." Heod straightened. "I reckon they wanted some cannon fodder. I'll work and be glad to." The other men murmured agreement.

A man covered in soot and oil lifted a hand. "Sorry ma'am, but I need to check on the engine. If it isn't shut down right, it'll damage her."

"Chiza, will you ask someone to supervise, one of the engine smiths would be best."

***

"I didn't realize that winning a battle would involve so much work." Llathia stretched and rolled her shoulders.

"Congu and Sombi and the other Harasahn countries will need to work hard to prove we aren't the savages that Kershia has made us out to be." Roger rocked kkitatin who'd refused to let go of him once he'd returned to the Mtuaka staal.

"I'm worried that the Lion isn't back."

"Trust Cal. She won't fly at night without cause, but I pity any Kershians who try to stand against her."

"She didn't seem that dangerous."

"The Kershians abducted her and forced her to work for them. She brought down their secret laboratory and buried it under a mountain. That was working alone."

"She didn't tell me that."

"I don't think she likes to think of it. It reminds her that she can't go home."

"I see. What do we do after this war is done?"

"We don't really want to fight a war but to defend our land. We won't take the fighting to Kershia. The world is changing, and we will need to change with it if we are to survive."

***

"Boilers hot, engines ready."

"Ask our friends to cast off," Cal ordered. Her heart lifted as the ship rose. *It isn't your ship.* That didn't stop her from enjoying the flight. The morning light shone into her eyes. Out of long habit, she narrowed her eyes. "If you aren't running an engine, keep a watch. It is a good practice even if we don't expect anything."

They floated through the cool air, not more than a hundred feet over the jungle, then over the river, turned gold by the morning light.

"Let's swing by the staal and see if the Lady Mtuaka is awake yet."

The occupants of the staal came out to stare at the Lion. Llathia came out and ordered a space cleared.

"Spilling air, keep the fires hot." The Lion touched down gently, and Cal jumped out. "Reporting in, the Sombi now control the mine. I told them they could keep it."

"You just gave the mine away? Just like that?" Roger came through the crowd, his lips twitching.

"They were ready to burn it all down. I explained the value of coal and since they were there, they might as well keep it going."

"King vvatha may have something to say about that."

"He can take a percentage of the coal for the kingdom. I might have hinted at something like that."

"Cal!" kkitatin ran up. "You're back. I want to go on the ship."

"You have to ask the Lady Mtuaka, it is her ship."

"Please?" kkitatin looked up at Llathia with big eyes.

"Hop on board and stay out of the way."

Before they returned to the cave, they tied the three Eagles to the gondola. Kkitatin stayed glued to the window for the entire short flight. Roger stood beside her grinning.

Llathia and Cal went over the ship carefully.

"Stock her up with ammunition and supplies," Cal suggested. "I've got an itch between my shoulders."

"Father has already been sending warriors in small groups to Biafa. Any we don't need to keep order here should head east." Roger said.

"The Sombi sent a runner. The engine driver is willing to drive his engine, Monsha is watching him. There's a flat car they brought the boats up on." Llathia said. "We could tie the Lion down and get her to the east without spending any water or coal."

"Good thinking." Cal stretched her shoulders. "Something tells me we don't have much time."

***

Commander Harkness looked through the spyglass.

"They certainly look like Kershian ships." He collapsed the glass. "Set a heading to parallel them, they'll turn for Hashan if they're heading for Sombi. They control the strait, so they don't have to pay the toll."

"What about the rumours of the Kershian sub-surface ship?" First Mate Samantha Coyne asked.

"We listen for strange pings and keep our distance. Orders are to observe only. We are not joining in battle under any circumstances. Neither the Kershians nor the Sombi can know we are present."

"Easier said than done," Samantha said, but she was already back at her station listening to the pings

"If it was easy, they'd have sent someone else."

Just as they approached the strait three days later, Samantha called out.

"Ship approaching, don't think she's on the surface."

"All hands to stations." Commander Harkness ordered.

"Sir, I'm hearing pings from another ship."

"Keep reporting as they approach. Batten her down, Switch to pressure ball. We're diving."

The crew worked in the dim electric light provided by a tiny generator that ran off the main engine.

"Main engine hot, fire doused and secure. Running smoothly." The engineer Adam Sweep reported.

"No unnecessary chatter; let Mate Coyne do her job."

"Other ship is still heading directly for us from our port side."

"Port rudder, let me know when we're head-on."

"Now, Commander."

"Straight ahead, steady as she goes."

"The other ship is still above us."

"What is the strongest length of our ship?" Harkness asked.

"We designed it to be the keel, sir."

"We did, didn't we. All hands hold fast, things are going to get rough. We are rolling the ship."

"Engineering fast."

"Ping station fast."

"Commander's station fast." Harkess strapped his harness tight to hold him in his chair.

"Flood port ballast, blow starboard ballast."

"The other ship has changed direction."

"Keep steady." They were at a ninety-degree angle. The chairs swivelled as they'd been designed to.

"Other ship passing in ten, nine, eight…"

"Hard starboard rudder," Harkness shouted. "Brace."

A horrendous scraping rang through the ship, a bang, then silence.

"Damage report."

"Buckling on the starboard beam, leaks but minor ones," Engineering responded. "Living quarters are flooding. Hatches holding."

"Mate, the heading of the other ship?"

"Unchanged sir, speed is decreasing. Still diving. I wonder if she damaged her prop and steering."

"Monitor their progress."

"Fading sir, their pings have stopped."

"Very well, set course to shadow the Kershian fleet. We'll pass through the strait after dark."

***

"Who is going to make all the money from this invasion?" Svan waved his beer mug. "I know it won't be me."

"They say the palace is full of gold for the taking." One of his drinking companions finished his mug. "Refill! I'm going to be stinking rich.

"You and every other guy on our ship, assuming you survive."

"What, you think these savages can give us a fight?"

"They kicked us out once already." Svan drew a pattern in a puddle on the table.

"They massacred our people and stole their land and weapons."

"And that is why the men who surrendered and were returned to Kershian were hung as deserters."

"Keep it down." One of the others looked around. "An officer hears you, you'll be in the brig."

"Why?" Svan leaned forward. "Why are we more afraid of our own officers than the enemy?"

"Won't be long now." The first one said. "A week and we'll be knee-deep in gold."

Chapter 21 Movement

Ttaoku scouted ahead his group from Kkittu down the river. The Sombi left markers for the Congu, but this was his old hunting grounds. The last few days most of the warriors from either side of the river had headed east.

"Movement ahead." Ddokna motioned. Ttaoku nodded and held up his hand for the warriors to wait, while he scouted out what was going on.

On the bank was a boat, larger than the barges, but smaller than any ocean fairing vessel. He signalled for Roger to come forward.

"What are they saying?" Ttaoku signed.

"Don't know why we got sent to the back end of nowhere. No gold up here." A younger looking Kershian said.

"S'pose to check on why the train is late." A grizzled one said. "Grunts don't get gold. You be good and I'll let you keep some coal from the train."

"So why have we stopped?"

"I saw a fruit tree somewhere round here. I'm tired of rations. The locals probably just dropped another tree on the track. It's not like there's a rush." They vanished into the jungle.

"Let's take the boat," Roger whispered. "They've got a cannon on the bow."

"How are we going to do that if there are more Kershians on board?" Ttaoku asked but slipped back to the rest of the group.

"Hey Sarge!" a man yelled from the boat. "Blast it, I'm coming onshore. I need to stretch me legs."

No answer came.

"I'm not joking. The ensign is getting ticked."

"Fine, fine, just be quick about it," Roger called.

Men poured off the boat, one refused, swearing and red-faced. It would have been an even battle if the men had carried their rifles ashore, but only a few older ones did. The Kkittu men jumped out of the greenery and the fight was over before it began. The only shot fired was Roger taking out the ensign.

"Collect any gear that might be useful, then get on the ship."

It was too crowded for all of them to get on board, so ddokna and Voz'ci picked ten warriors and ttaoku was to lead the rest of the group east.

"Stay sharp, if there is one boat, there could be another," Roger said. "We'll go slow, try to keep up."

***

Roger steered the boat, ddokna ran the engine, no more complicated than the barges, just a bit bigger. They chugged downstream until he saw smoke rising over the trees ahead.

"Does that look like too much smoke there?" Roger asked

Voz'ci nodded so Roger pulled over to the bank and whistled. Half an hour later ttaoku waved at him.

"I'm thinking enemy activity at the village ahead. Go ahead, surround the place, but don't attack unless I signal, or they see you and fire at you."

"Got it." He faded back into the jungle.

He heard the shooting before they saw the village.

"Full ahead!" Roger shouted. "Arm yourselves but stay out of sight for the moment."

They rounded the bend to see the village smouldering, a squad of Kershians backed toward another boat.

"Get ready," Roger ordered. "Fire on my command."

The warriors lined up in the bow, kneeling with their rifles aiming over the side.

One of the Kershians saw them and waved to for them to shoot toward the village.

"Ready." Roger said, "One quarter ahead."

A shout came from the other boat, Roger couldn't hear the words, but the squad swivelled and aimed at them.

"Fire at will."

The guns barked and blue smoke obscured his vision. A bullet came through the glass and hit somewhere behind him. They kept firing and more bullets came through the window. He saw a shadow through the smoke jump up to the cannon. It boomed and the boat rocked. The firing stopped. When he'd passed out of the cloud Roger could see the other boat sinking before it exploded. The boiler must have gone.

He pulled up beside the remnants of the other boat.

Ttaoku came out of the village, his jaw set.

"Sorry, my lord, but once the men saw what went on in the village, I ordered them to attack."

"What's done is done," Roger said. "Casualties?"

Calliope and the Engine Smith

"Two dead, another three with injuries, claim they are just flesh wounds."

"And the villagers?"

"All dead from what we could see, even the women and children."

"You did the right thing."

In the end, they found two children hiding in a chicken coop.

"We bring them with us until we find their clan."

"Roger," Voz'ci said softly. "A couple of the men think they can recover the cannon and shells from the other boat."

"Have people standing by with rifles in case the crocodiles come. The rest will put the village to rest."

The next day they left behind the still smouldering village. Ttaoku and another man were working at mounting the second cannon so they could use both without them banging into each other.

"I want the cannons loaded and men at the bow ready. If there are two boats, there will be three."

***

Petor cursed his luck. While the navy had an easy trip to the Sombi port, they were told to march from the desert kingdom. First it was desert, then mountains, and now this ocean of tall grass. The men walked in three files and close enough that they could see the man in front of them.

"Creeps me out," Hans in the file beside Petor said. "I heard there are little people live in the grass."

"If they're that little we'll have no problems.

They stopped and cut a circle in the grass for a camp for the night. Ten men were missing. They set a double watch, marching around the camp in opposite directions, half carrying guns and half torches.

"Too bad we can't burn the whole thing." Hans was carrying the gun.

"Right, light a fire in the middle of this hell hole." Petor snorted. "Smart."

Petor had the last watch before the morning. The sun seemed to leap into the sky and the men got up and started to pack the camp. Ten men were slow to get up. When the sergeant gave one a kick, the man flopped lifelessly. All ten were dead

"We walk until we're out of this place." The captain ordered. "Stay within sight of the men in front of you. Stay sharp, watch out for each other."

As the sun travelled through the sky men vanished, or simply fell over dead, a dart in their neck. Petor walked trying to look in all directions. He looked over at Hans, and his companion was gone. A rustle in the tall grass caught his attention he brought up his gun and stepped forward. Whatever was there was gone. Petor turned to go back to the column, and it was gone. He ran in circles trying to find the trail left by the marching men.

"Hey!" he shouted. "I'm out here. Anyone there?"

A tiny man appeared in front of him. He could have walked under Petor's outstretched arm without ducking. Petor lifted his gun and fired, and the man fell to the ground. Petor laughed. They could die. He would kill them all, then burn the grass.

Something pricked his chest and he looked down to see an absurdly small arrow sticking out of him. He pulled it out, then another hit him, and a third. Petor spun around to see where they were coming from. He fired into the grass, but the arrows kept hitting him. Black spots danced in his eyes, and he fell to his knees. The tiny man stood over him, then took Petor's gun and bullet case. Others poked at him, but he couldn't do anything but lie there, staring up into the sun in the blue sky.

***

The idea of putting the Lion on the flatbed seemed good, but in practice, it was a nightmare. In the end, they floated the airship then winched the gondola down into place. Deflating the envelope and packing it safely took longer than getting the gondola settled.

While llathia supervised packing the Lion and Monsha and the warriors cleaned out the carriages, Cal went over the engine with the driver.

"We're gonna need some coal," Henrei the driver said. "Water too. Fastest to go up to the mine."

"We'll need to take Monsha with us. They won't know we have the train."

With Henrei's help, they decoupled the engine and coal car.

"We should be back by nightfall."

They were greeted by the same man as before. "You told us we owned the mine."

"That's right, I did," Cal said through Monsha. "What do you want to trade for the coal?"

"We want a working engine."

"Do you have one that isn't working?"

"This way." Jjono, the Sombi who'd met them led her to the mine.

An engine was connected to a huge spool of cable. Cal found a few greasy tools and dove into the engine. It mostly needed cleaning and oiling. She was covered in oil and grease when Monsha showed up.

"You're just in time." Cal greeted him. "Can you translate for me?" She explained how to run and maintain the engine. "When all this is done, I'll come back and train you properly."

They took the now filled and prepared railway engine back down to the village.

"We're ready to go," llathia took Cal on a walk around of the Lion one last time while the warriors piled onto the carriages.

When they got to the grassland, they stopped the train.

"I don't know if anyone is there to hear me, but the Sombi have reclaimed the railway. When you are ready, we will talk." Llathia climbed back into the carriage, and they continued on the way east. The farm country looked deserted, and Cal thought about the Kershians up in Kkittu. She hoped the fighting didn't make its way to this peaceful landscape.

They parked the train in sight of the city, they could see a steady flow of people from the city.

"Looks like trouble." Llathia frowned. "Monsha take some people and see if you can find out what is happening."

Chapter 22 Biafa

The Sombi officers gathered around the king. The lushly decorated room contrasting with the utilitarian warrior gear "They will think they can simply waltz in and take over." King vvatha thumped on the table. "We're going to make them regret their arrogance."

"What if they land and go around the city?" a general asked.

"They will try to cut to the heart of the country. Control Biafa, control Sombi."

"Despite the Kershians holding the railway and the west?"

"Why invade territory they already hold?" King vvatha leaned back, "But you may warn warriors from the outlying areas and get them on watch. The Congu will help hold the coast between us and Lusundi. The coast north of here is inhospitable."

"I've heard rumours that the Congu have kicked the Kershians out of the east." Another general said.

"If it is true, that is good news, but it can't change our plans here.

"So who is going to tell the people in the city?" Ssyache asked.

"You organize the city guard to spread the word."

***

Ssyache muttered under his breath as they walked through the district knocking on doors explaining to people how the evacuation would work.

"Take what you can carry. We've set up camps outside the city, but unless you love rice and beans, remember to bring food."

He'd said the same thing so many times, answered the same question so many times. He could have repeated it in his sleep; in fact, his wife complained that he did.

King vvatha's plan to empty Biafa and turn it into a trap for the Kershians was both daring and frighteningly risky. The last week had been spent putting the King's wishes into action. He should have known better than to speak up.

"I'll take the risk and stay." A grandmother said arms crossed. "That is your choice, but you will spend the time in the cells for disobeying a direct order from the King."

The days went past, and the city was spooky without people in the streets and markets. Even the poorer neighbourhoods went for the free food.

"Ships sighted." A runner sprinted past.

"Let's get to our positions."

"Ssyache, the train has stopped a few miles from the city." Another runner came.

"Anybody get off the train?"

"Sombi warriors."

"Run back, tell them ships have been sighted. Ask them to defend the camp. It's too late to coordinate them with our people."

***

Roger looked at the expanse of the ocean. They stopped to talk to Congu warriors who had paddled across the river and showed them the boat so they knew its weakness.

"It's just a machine, it isn't impervious, put a hole in it and it will sink. A spear or bow will kill a Kershian as easy as a bullet."

"Yes, Third Prince."

"We'll follow the coastline and let people know you're coming. We want to be fighting Kershians, not each other. The rest of our people will work with you to show cooperation is possible."

The swell of the ocean made the boat rock gently.

"Roger, are those ships?" Voz'ci pointed.

"Airships." He scanned the horizon. "The navy won't be far away. I hope we get there in time. We can't do much against the big ships, but we can slow down any landing craft. Let's put on some steam."

***

They chugged along the coast until they saw smoke on the horizon.

"We stop, we may not make it to Biafa in time, but we can help the people here."

Gunfire sounded across the waves.

"We need to distract them, get them focused on us, not the villagers." Roger went to the cannon. "Voz'ci take the other one. Aim for their ship"

Aiming with the movement of the boat was impossible, so Roger chose to get as close as possible to the other ship. Soon they were getting return fire. The other ship was docked and could aim more accurately.

"Get close to shore, rifles on the left side. Fire at anyone in uniform."

Water splashed over them, but the shells continued to miss even if only by a few feet. Voz'ci landed a shot on the other ship, then another. Gunfire from shore buzzed past them. Roger aimed for the other boat's cannon, waiting to time the shot. A shell struck the rail beside him as he fired.

***

Voz'ci caught Roger as he fell to the deck. The other ship's bow exploded, and the firing from the ship stopped.

Blood seeped from a wound in Roger's side. "Get him inside, keep shooting." Voz'ci went back to the cannon and hammered the other ship to make sure there would be no more fire from them.

War shouts came from the jungle and then gunfire. The Kershians on the beach dropped their guns and knelt on the sand.

"Do not kill anyone who has surrendered." Ttaoku bellowed to the shore. A Congu man walked out of the foliage unarmed, hands spread.

"We are here to help." He shouted in accented Sombi.

"Come on," a man yelled.

The boat grounded and Ttaoku jumped over the side.

"Move away from your guns." He yelled at the Kershians in Sombi. One of the Kershians said something to his men, then yelled the same thing loudly. Other Kershians came out of the village hands up, followed by Sombi and Congu carrying spears and bows.

"We have injured," Ttaoku said. "Is there a healer in the village?"

"We have one with us." The Congu said and waved forward another man. "C'hahb, help them out, then anyone else who needs it."

"May we rescue any injured on our ship?" The Kershian asked in heavily accented Sombi.

"We will send people to check your comrades."

***

Roger woke up to an agonizing pain in his right arm and lesser hurts scattered about his body.

"Good, you're conscious." The Congu leaning over him looked vaguely familiar.

"Who?"

"I'm a healer, my prince. I'm from the Hrona clan, we've met briefly before."

"Ah, in good hands."

"Drink some of this, not too quickly." C'hahb held a cup to Roger's lips. "It is powerful, you need to sleep for a while longer. We, and the village, are safe. The Kershians surrendered. I must go, I have others to attend to."

The next time Roger woke, the pain was distanced from him. He knew it was there, but it didn't impact him. C'hahb and an old Sombi woman were deep in discussion about herbs and roots, though neither spoke the other's language.

"Are you up to hear a report?" Voz'ci sat beside Roger's mat.

"I am."

"Aside from your injury, another man died from rifle fire. Fifteen warriors were injured or killed in the village. The Kershians have twenty injured or dead. The explosion on the ship killed everyone still on board. Ddokna has taken the ship with ttaoku and two other warriors. He didn't think the rifles would do much against navy ships."

"How long asleep?"

"Two days, what is going to happen in Biafa has happened."

Roger nodded carefully.

"Other villages?"

"We haven't heard of other invasions. Scouts are out checking between here and Biafa."

"Stay alert, we don't know what will happen there.

"Of course, my prince."

***

A runner came up to the train, gasping for air.

"Ships in sight." He put his hands on his knees.

"Make ready to launch," Llathia shouted. She'd ordered the boilers to be kept hot if not up to full pressure, which added to the challenge of transporting the balloons, they ended up rolling them and hanging them over the side of the gondola.

"Eagle warriors check your wings," Cal said. "Loosen all the ropes but the corners. Let's get the envelope in place."

Llathia kissed Chiza. "You're in command, my love."

"Any warrior not boarding the ship, let's go with the runner and make ourselves useful."

When the Lion lifted, the warriors cheered.

"We're flying high," Llathia said. "It will get cold, keep moving, don't stiffen up. Prepare yourself for battle."

Chapter 23 The Clash Begins

Llathia ordered a watch to the east as they rose.

"Engines half ahead. Steady as she goes."

They passed over Biafa, already tiny below them, then their shadow crossed onto the blue ocean. The sun was high in the sky, so the shadow would only betray them if directly overhead.

"Ships spotted." Monsha pointed. "Those have to be the airships to be visible from this far."

"Do we go to meet them or wait?"

"My advice would be to wait. We don't want to get too far from friendly shores." Cal looked up from checking the disc throwers.

"Very well, we soar like the eagles, then pounce."

The three airships grew faster than llathia expected.

"Those are huge, I've never seen anything like them." Llathia's heart pounded.

"They have to be the size of the Adamant. Remember most of that size is air."

"But they'd be able to lift a crew of twenty."

"Probably lifting cannons rather than extra people. That's what I'd do. Don't know how well they did with the pressure ball since I left their company, so they could be steam cannons. I wouldn't want gunpowder near the hydrogen."

"Hydrogen?" Llathia asked to distract from her nerves.

"A very light gas, it allows them to stay aloft without burning coal, but it burns very quickly."

"Looks like they are beginning to separate."

186

"It's time. Port engine one-quarter speed, let's get over them."

Suddenly the ships seemed to move at a glacial pace. She kept waiting for some sign they'd been spotted.

"Spilling air, stand by on the ballast." Llathia focused on the battle.

The Kershian airships grew at a frightening rate.

"They'll be compartmentalized, one back won't knock them try to throw out the bags just before we cross over their path," Cal said and grabbed a bag.

"Drop on Cal's command," Llathia ordered.

"Drop one…drop two…three…" She pushed the bag through the hole in the floor.

"We're dropping too fast! Dump ballast."

"If the eagles fly, that will help." Monsha dropped a bag through the floor.

"Eagles away, try to land on the same ship and take her over."

The centre ship's balloon ruffled, and it tilted toward the bow. The others turned and rose to meet them.

Monsha and his companions climbed out the windows and dropped away. For a horrifying moment, llathia thought they weren't going to grab air, but before they shrank to nothing, the tiny flecks appeared soaring in circles over their prey.

"They are Eagles in truth." Llathia boasted. "I want to get between and above the ships, whichever one Monsha takes, we'll attack the other."

"More ballast away, we're still too fast, we'll drop below them at this rate." Cal heaved more bags off the ship.

"Monsha is over the south ship, we'll take the north. Port engine half ahead, starboard one quarter ahead, now, both engines reverse."

"Hold on for impact," Cal shouted, "secure the fires."

They hit the Kershian ship's envelope to the starboard side and tilted sharply. One of the warriors working the disc throwers was tossed hard against the wall and didn't move.

"Portside discs." The wooden plates hit the fabric of the enemy ship and bounced off. Then the ships separated, and they were firing discs at the Kershian gondola. They hit the wood and splintered it, at least one hit a window. Then they were below the enemy ship, but they'd slowed their descent hitting the envelope.

"Port propeller damaged," Hovid reported. "Don't know if it will hold out to even half power."

"Noted. Starboard engine half ahead. Ease on the power on the port side. Stop when you must. Let's get behind them."

***

Ssyache watched the airship soar over the city rising rapidly into the blue sky. He shouted a war cry which the others took up. They didn't have a lot of time to celebrate, the enemy was coming fast, and they had three huge ships and five or six smaller ones.

"Remember your orders," Ssyache told his men, though he couldn't do anything about the other squads scattered through the eastern half of the city.

"One of the enemy airships is in trouble."

"We've fired the first shot; it remains to be seen who gets the last."

The two bigger ships hung back, the third big ship turning broadside to the port.

"That canny old man called it," Ssyache whispered as if the king might be listening over his shoulder.

The first shots landed short of the pier and his men laughed, but they moved closer to the shore with each shot. Then one hit a warehouse knocking down half the building. If they bombarded the whole city, it would be a disaster. The king counted on them wanting to keep Biafa in usable condition.

"Don't panic, don't get excited, we're just getting started," Ssyache said.

It made him sick to see the port be destroyed. It was ancient, the heart of the Sombi nation.

Better the port than the people. The chore of evacuating the city didn't seem so bad in retrospect. For now, all they could do was watch and curse.

***

Ttaoku stared at the ships. He thought he'd seen big ships from Locossia, but these were monstrous, though only one was firing on the city.

"We have to help, but we can't go up against that gunship."

"What if we put up the Kershian colours, they're on a shelf below. We might be able to tackle the small ones. Look how they are holding the big one in place."

"So be it, as the Congu would say, it will be a hunt to be told." He drove the little riverboat out toward the fleet, praying they got to fire at least one shot before they died. One of the smaller boats steamed over toward them.

A man with gold braid on his uniform came out to shout at them, then soldiers ran to the side with their guns ready.

"Shoot the one who's yelling," Ttaoku said. "Been an honour, we will arrive in the afterlife with no debt on our soul."

"Don't be too quick to get to the afterlife." Ddokna laughed and fired the cannon, hitting the deck where the man in braid was standing. The other soldiers were thrown back. They pulled up close to the bigger ship as the soldiers scrambled to get back into position. He fired again scattering them.

Their boat bumped into the bigger one and the man beside ddokna fired the cannon point black at the waterline of the other boat. The blast pushed him back, but he struggled to his feet, blood running from his ears. His partner loaded the cannon and they fired again. Water poured through the hole as frenzied shouting came from above where the soldiers had to lean out to try to shoot them.

Ttaoku fired back as fast as he could load his gun. He didn't hit many, but it kept them from aiming.

Ddokna lined up his cannon with the edge of the ship and fired. Screams and curses fell on them. Then a muffled thump shook the ship, and the soldier ran away.

"Let's get on the ship. It has bigger guns." Ddokna shouted. Ttaoku shrugged and tossed a grappling hook on a rope over the top of the ship where it lodged. He swarmed up the rope, followed by Ddokna and the other two. On the other side of the ship sailors and soldiers filled two small boats as they rowed away as fast as they could.

"Time to play with the big gun. It took a minute for ddokna to figure out the crank to swing the guns about and another raise or lower the muzzle.

"Just like our cannons but bigger," Ddokna shouted as he opened the breach and stuffed a cartridge in and closed it. He cranked the gun around to point at the stern of the huge ship. "Fire!"

Chapter 24 Locked in Combat

The exhilaration of flight captured Monsha for a brief time as they plummeted toward their target. When he caught air, the relief hit him like a drug, and he laughed in delight. It didn't matter that he was headed toward a deadly fight, this was what he was born to do.

The challenge was to time their landing, so they didn't simply bounce off the balloon. Unlike the Lion, it had a rigid shell, so they didn't have to worry about collapsing the balloon and suffocating.

He landed and dropped out of the Eagle, making it fast before he looked for his companions. All of them had landed safely.

"We are in a battle, do not hesitate."

"Will the rope be long enough?" N'kom asked.

"We will attach one rope at a time, be careful, you only get to slip once." Monsha tied off one end of his rope near the centre of the huge ship and led the way over the side. The netting on the outside of the balloon helped until the balloon curved underneath and they dangled over empty space.

"If we get inside the netting it would be easier," Vom'xa suggested. "We cut a couple of pieces we should be able to slip inside."

"Good thinking." Monsha locked his feet on the rope and used the short spear on his back to hack away at the thick webbing. When the last strand parted the web stretched enough for him to crawl through. They moved down the ropes like spiders on a huge tree until they reached the gondola.

"We must be swift and silent. There is no telling how many of their warriors are on board." Monsha pointed to the trap door. "N'kom and I will go forward, you move to the rear and take the engines. We want a working ship, so try not to break too much."

He pried the door open with his spear and looked down. A man stood looking bored beside cannons. Monsha dropped through the trap door and clubbed the man. The other three joined him, they tied and gagged the Kershian and peered briefly at the cannon. The rumble of engines came through the wall.

"Once we own the ship, we can worry about how they work." Vom'xa went to one of the two doors and opened it a crack. He signalled that there was another man in the next space, then flung open the door and threw his spear, killing the man instantly. The others followed, Monsha pointed toward another door, he cracked it open and peeked through. A man in a fancy uniform was turning a wheel. Monsha guessed it was to steer the ship. It looked easier than balancing two engines constantly. Two others were in the room with a huge window looking out over Biafa. He closed the door.

"Three men, all looking out the window. N'kom, you take the other door." Monsha pointed. The others moved to the opposite door.

Monsha counted to ten, then burst through the door. The three men spun to stare at him. The one in the fancy uniform reached for the gun on his belt, but Monsha crossed the distance between them in three long strides and thrust his spear through the man's heart. He spun to take the other two, but N'kom had already taken them down, one was obviously dead, the other was unconscious, bleeding from a head wound.

That was when gunshots came from the rear of the ship.

***

The Lion dropped to the rear of the Kershian ship and below. They tried firing more discs, but they didn't have enough angle. A puff of steam came from the other ship, but they didn't feel anything hit the Lion.

"Engines, full heat to the balloon, one quarter ahead." They dropped farther back, then started rising again. Something shook the Lion and Llathia waited for them to fall into the ocean. They continued to rise.

The other ship was closing in on them, so Cal and Hishka took to the disc throwers on that side.

"Don't try to hit the gondola, take out more of their balloon," Cal said as she sent her first disc soaring away.

Llathia turned her attention back to the ship in front of her. They were rising too, and faster than the Lion. They were turning to bring their cannons to bear, and faster than Llathia had thought possible.

"Starboard half ahead, port full stop." The maneuver brought the other ship into range of the discs but left them open to attack by the damaged ship.

"Hishka, take the disc throwers on the other side, put some holes in that ship."

She ran across to the other side and started firing discs. More shots came from the other ship, hitting the envelope and the webbing. The Lion tilted to the port side, putting the damaged ship out of range but opening the ship beside them to the discs.

Another puff of steam and a bang. Something smashed through the starboard wall and out the port.

"Cal, get some ballast off the ship, we need to get higher," Llathia said. "Both engines one half ahead."

"Don't know if the port propeller will take it," Hovid replied.

"Do the best you can then."

Llathia's face ached, then she realized she was smiling. This was a much larger arena, but the stakes were the same, only one of them would survive. All other concerns were irrelevant.

The other ships weren't firing. The Lion was between them and though it was an easy target, they risked hitting each other.

"We need to do as much damage as we can, right now."

Hishka tossed a disc toward Hovid. "Get it burning."

He pushed it into the firebox and paused in his feeding coal to the fire. Then he scraped it out kicked the disc back to her. She used a spear and a knife to load the glowing disc, then fired it before it lit the Lion on fire.

It burned as it flew between the ships but dropped below the balloon to roar past the front window of the other ship.

It dropped ballast and rose faster, moving out of range.

Cal shoved a handful of discs into the firebox on her side and took the tongs from Shisnak.

"Use tongs to load the discs." She pulled one out of the firebox, loading it and firing it in one motion.

The disc sailed away, and Cal was already loading the next one to fire it.

Another ball smashed through the back of the Lion's gondola, and it began to twist as it moved.

"One-quarter engines!" Llathia yelled.

The next ball hit near the port engine, and it sagged through the floor.

"Hovid get out of there."

He jumped for the other side of the gondola as the engine tumbled out of the Lion, driving the port propeller into the webbing. It shredded but cut some of the rope holding the gondola in place causing the ship to creak and twist.

"Cal, can you see Hovid?" Llathia called.

"No, I'm sorry."

Llathia looked through the hole in the floor of the ship but knew it was useless. Far below the engine splashed into the ocean.

The entire port side of the ship was in shreds. Hishka clung to her disc thrower on the tilting bit of floor. The other one on that side had vanished with the engine.

Free of the weight of the engine, the Lion shot upwards out of range of the cannons from the still undamaged ship. They were almost directly above the wounded vessel.

"Cal, can you finish that ship with the steam cannon?" Llathia asked

"Can try." Cal moved carefully to the stern of the gondola and pressurized the cannon.

Firing the steam cannon shook the ship and made it protest, but the already damaged ship tilt almost sixty degrees to the bow, then Llathia saw the flames as the ship came apart and fell to the ocean near one of the tiny ships.

"Too bad it didn't land on the ship."

Hishka had crawled over to the starboard side and taken over the disc thrower. She started firing them at the ship below them.

"I'm going to stay above that ship. Let's try to knock it down." Llathia said, but all they could do was sail in an ever-larger circle and hope they happened to pass over the other ship.

***

The ship shook with the blast of the gun and ddokna covered his ears to try to stop the ringing. Their small boat was chugging away toward another gunship. They loaded the gun again and fired it. This time ddokna was prepared for the bang and watched as the ocean beside the big gunship splashed near the tugboat. Ttaoku helped crank the gun over a bit, then loaded and fired again. The splash was so close to the tug that ddokna hoped they'd damaged it. Ttaoku cranked it a bit as Ddokna grabbed a shell to load.

This shot hit the tug and it listed to the side.

A splash near them reminded Ddokna they were in the middle of a battle.

Their small boat was driving straight toward the gunship, firing steadily from the cannons. It looked like a kitten taking on a Lion.

"Over there." Ttaoku pointed at where the last small ship was firing at them. They had to crank the gun through more than ninety degrees to get close to the ship. In the meantime, the enemy had zeroed in on them and shells landed all around them. The deck was underwater as they fired, reloaded, and cranked the gun around to fire again. They were lucky and hit the ship in the middle. Ddokna loaded and they fired again as a shell struck near them, the force throwing them over the side. The other ship was smoking, and they'd stopped firing. They couldn't see their small boat from the water, but the firing of the cannons had stopped.

"Looks like we're swimming," Ttaoku said and grabbed onto a box floating near them.

Ddokna took the other side. "It was fun while it lasted."

The big ships behind the huge gunship were heading toward the shore, one of them coming straight at them. They were slowing to pick up people in the rowboats who'd escaped from the sinking ship.

"Let's head that way, maybe we can catch one of the boats when they're done with it."

***

Ssyache saw the small boat get hit and the big gunship drifted enough that they weren't bombarding the port. The ships on either side of them steamed forward and his heart sank.

"Those are full of soldiers." Ssayche pointed at them. "I don't know if we have enough bullets to kill them all, but we need to convince them we do."

He led his team forward through the rubble of the port to where they could see the ship ram into the dock and lower a bridge for soldiers to pour out of in Biafa.

"Make every shot count," Ssyache ordered them.

They dropped a few men before the ones on the dock formed a line and started shooting back. Then the line fell apart as another Sombi group opened fire from close by. The dock became a lethal space as they shot at each other. The Kershians weren't concerned with running out of ammunition and peppered everything close to them with lead. Ssyache picked his targets, and any other day would have been happy with hitting half of them from this distance. Today it wasn't good enough. The Kershian formed more lines and kept up the barrage.

"Retreat and we'll take our second position."

Crawling through the rubble with bullets zinging overhead was slow going, but once they got out of the line of fire, they ran to the building where they could lie on the roof and shoot at anyone coming through the rubble.

Ssyache looked over and saw the second big ship steaming toward the shore on the other side of the bay. They didn't have as many people over there as the king didn't think they could land a ship on that side.

"They're too far away for us to do anything."

Kershians were coming through the rubble taking shelter from gunmen on the ground but not thinking about taller buildings.

"Fire at will and make it count." Ssayche peered down the barrel and pulled the trigger.

***

Monsha took the leader's gun, the other two weren't armed, and told N'kom to steer toward the other ship. He slipped through the door, expecting bullets to tear through him, but the room was empty but for the corpse of the Kershian gunner.

The door to the back was half open and a man was peering around. So at least one of the others was still alive. Monsha lined up his shot, but the gun kicked more than he expected, and bullet pinged on the boiler behind the man with the gun. He adjusted for the kick and aimed again, but the other man spun to fire and Monsha ducked out of the way. A chunk of wall flew out over his head.

Monsha heard a babble of shouting on the other side of the door. He ran through crouched over to see Vox'ma standing behind the gunman holding a spear he'd stabbed through the man's back. His partner lay unmoving on the floor. Two Kershians crouched with hands over their heads.

"Surrender." One said in a strange Sombi accent. And ducked his head like he expected to be shot.

"Attack and you're dead." Monsha waved the gun and they nodded vigorously.

"Vom'xa tie these two up over there." Monsha pointed. "Then go see if you can figure out the cannons. Tell N'kom I will run the engine."

Monsha looked at them. At first, it was overwhelming, but under the wheels and valves, it wasn't much different from the one they'd repurposed for the Lion. He could do this.

Chapter 25 Last Stand

They drifted away from the other Kershian ship and Cal pointed down.

"We need to stop that troopship before it lands."

"How?" We only have one engine." Llathia asked.

"Spill the air like you did over the jungle, if nothing else we can crash into them and hope the boiler blows."

They dropped past the enemy ship and the other one Monsha had chosen to attack. Cal fired the steam cannon praying the bolts at least came close enough to scare the people on the ship.

The ship below them was too huge to be sunk by the pinpricks she was sending their way.

"Llathia, let's get up to the balloon and cut the ship free. A boiler explosion might damage the ship enough"

They climbed up onto the roof of the gondola and tied themselves to the webbing, then chopped away at the ropes with the axes llathia insisted on for standard equipment.

"Faster, or we'll miss the ship." Llathia hacked and slashed until the gondola dropped from under her leaving only a few ropes holding. Cal swung on her rope to catch the walls of the ship and climbed up to cut the last rope. She was too focused to worry about the amount of air between her and the ocean with nothing to catch her. She couldn't help but laugh as the Lion tumbled out of the sky.

Cal was sure they'd missed, even the huge ship was a small target given the size of the ocean. Then the gondola crashed

202

through the top deck of the ship. A puff of steam was the engine, then a heavier thump as the pressure ball blew. The ship broke in half and tiny specks filled the water. Cal knew in her mind each one was a person, but they were too far away to tug at her conscience.

With the weight of the gondola and engine gone, their drop slowed to a gentle drift. They were out of the battle unless they chose to throw the axes they held.

And the big gunship was still untouched. Cal climbed the rope until she could lock her feet and take the weight off the harness. Llathia did the same thing. The remainder of the crew followed their example

"How did you become an engine smith?" Cal asked.

"My father built an engine to run a sawmill. I learned by helping him maintain it. Then the Third Prince asked me to build him an engine. My father's mill exploded, my mother survived, she works in my kitchen.

"Things got political, and I ended up fighting N'toox in the arena. Chiza and I were the only ones who thought I had any chance of surviving. N'toox was as nasty a human being as I've ever met, I don't feel guilt for killing him, it was his own certainty he'd win that allowed it."

"You sound like me. I would have been happy to mess around with engines and drawing for the rest of my life, but important people decided I had potential and suddenly I was building airships and arguing with admirals."

"Roger told me you blew up a mountain."

"The Kershians grabbed me, I may have overdone it a bit."

They talked about their lives until a flaming airship fell past them and reminded them there was a battle on.

***

N'kom screamed in rage when the gondola fell and called for full power to get vengeance for their engine smith. Monsha pushed the engine, but the airship lumbered slowly across the sky. Too slow for his need he pushed on the wheel as if it would make the ship move faster.

The other Kershian airship headed for the city.

"Monsha, join Vom'xa and destroy that ship as we pass by."

Monsha yelled his agreement.

They flew past and hammered the ship with their cannons. The prisoners cowered in their corner as the weapons roared, not much different than the cannons the engineer had built. The ship broke apart and burst into flame then plummeted to the ocean far below.

"There is still the big gunship." Monsha came onto what Cal called the bridge. "Vom'xa is handling the engine for the moment. Let's go die gloriously."

They moved toward the ground heading for the ship.

"Turn around. Get under that balloon." N'kom shouted and pointed.

Monsha spun the wheel and they turned around ponderously. The balloon slid over the top of the envelope and fell curling and tumbling to the ocean.

"Go back on course, I'll return." N'kom ran from the bridge and Monsha put him out of his mind. If he crashed the airship into the navy vessel would that do enough damage? The airship was bigger but was all air and gossamer. He didn't see any other choice. He lined up the ship and steeled himself not to panic at the end.

"Just before you hit the ship, throw her hard to starboard and we'll try to take out the bridge. That's the big window on the high part of the ship.

Impossibly Cal came on the bridge and pointed ahead.

"Thanks for picking us up." The engine smith said. "It was a pleasant surprise." Hishna and Shisnak stood grinning behind them.

He stepped aside for the engine smith to take the wheel, but she shook her head.

"This is your ship. I'll help Cal with the cannon."

Monsha grinned ferociously. "Yes, Engine Smith."

They were close enough to see crew members on the gunship waving at them. Monsha spun the wheel and then was sure he was too late; they were going to crash after all.

***

Cal let the cannon overpressure by what she thought was a safe margin. Maybe the Kershians had learned about safety from her. She hoped.

The ship began to turn, and Cal got ready, she'd only get one shot at this.

The people on the bridge waved, frowned, or stepped back as the airship almost scraped the glass.

"Now," Llathia ordered, and Cal triggered the cannon. The ball smashed through the glass and the people on the bridge were tossed aside as if from a giant's hand. Then they were past, and Cal reloaded the cannon.

"C'mon, c'mon." She aimed the cannon at the base of the biggest gun and fired. The ball bounced off like a ball bearing against a rock. The gun swivelled to aim at them, and the airship was too slow to avoid the shot.

The cannon fired and exploded, if the shell came out of the barrel at all it missed their ship.

"Bring her around for another shot," Llathia yelled, and Cal loaded the cannon a third time. The airship turned slowly then Cal shouted in disbelief.

"Bring her around and hold her over the ship."

The ship's whistle almost deafened them, but what had Cal's attention was the white flag and the crew standing with hands in the air.

When they were over the ship, Cal slid down a rope to the deck.

A man in a black and gold uniform with blood oozing from a cut on his head met her.

"Accept our surrender and let us pick up our people in the water."

"If a gun so much as twitches we will shoot."

"No one will disobey." The man's shout was impressive.

"Keep signalling retreat," Cal said. The ship's whistle interrupted her. "Kill the engines and put the rescue boats in the water."

The man shouted at a nearby sailor who dashed off and minutes later the vibration of the engines stopped.

***

Ssyache picked his targets and shot conserving his shrinking amount of ammunition. Something fell on the other ship and sank it. The harbour filled with soldiers swimming for the shore or helping their comrades. They wouldn't be a threat without guns or bullets.

The last Kershian airship dropped from the sky and sailed past the big gunship. The boom of the cannon made him miss his shot and he reloaded and shot his man. Then another explosion put him off his aim. He reached for another cartridge and the bag was empty.

Someone waved a white flag on the big ship and the whistle blew at a painful volume. The soldiers coming through the rubble stopped and began to retreat.

"Hold your fire," Ssyache ordered.

"No fire left to hold," someone said.

"I don't know what is going on, but we're not going to make them attack again."

"Got no problem with that."

The ship with its nose stuck on the shore backed away, the ramp closing, and it steamed toward the broken ship in the harbour.

***

Chiza ordered his soldier into a line between the refugees and the city.

"A group of enemy approaching from the north." A runner came over after what felt like hours after they heard gunshots from the other side of the city.

"How many?"

"Four hands at least."

"We'll surround them, but don't let them see you. If they look like they're attacking, take them out."

Chiza led his men on the hunt, there wasn't a lot of cover, but there was enough to hide from people who weren't looking for them.

Just as the group of ragged men walked into their circle, a whistle came from the harbour. An argument broke out in the group and the leader shot one of his own people, then pointed at the defenceless refugees and lifted his gun.

"Now!" Chiza roared, he jumped up and threw his first spear which impaled the leader, the others died as quickly. The whistle kept blowing and no more enemy showed up and Chiza went from worrying about attackers to worrying about llathia.

***

Svan pulled the soldier out of the water and went back for another. He'd been rescuing his fellow Kershians since the ship broke in half and dumped them into the water. Exhaustion dragged at him, but there were so many who still needed help.

Halfway to the crowd of men struggling to stay afloat, he caught a mouthful of water and choked. He didn't have the strength to swim and cough at the same time.

Just as he sank under the water a hard grip pulled him to the surface. Svan didn't understand what the Harasahn man said, but he hauled himself into the boat as they rowed over to rescue the next person. He lay in the boat looking at the blue sky and wondered if the situation was reversed if he would have helped the black men.

CHAPTER 26 NEGOTIATION

Stopping the fighting took the rest of the day. Some Kershians immediately laid down their weapons, but others were too caught up in fighting. It didn't help that the Sombi also didn't know they could stop. On top of that, some of the Kershians took up looting whatever buildings were close to them, and it took Kershian military to put a stop to it.

Cal was exhausted by the time ssyache commanded she attend King vvatha and take part in the negotiations.

The room where the king and the Kershian general met was deceptively plain. A closer look showed gold veins through the stone of the floor and exotic wood making up the panelling.

"Cal Hrona Xanachi Shillingworth." She introduced herself in Kershian and Sombi then fell into a chair. "I have no official right to be part of this discussion other than your invitation."

"We are looking for the Third Prince and haven't located him yet. As his First Wife, it is your duty to speak on his behalf."

"Very well, but anything I negotiate must be ratified by Prince Roger or his father when it comes to issues affecting Congu. I assume King vvatha can negotiate on his own behalf for Sombi."

The king gave her a sour look but didn't say anything.

"I am General Mizvrat." He looked even more tired than Cal. "Normally negotiations would be in the language of the victors, but my Sombi is limited and my Congu non-existent. The emperor will need to agree to any final settlement."

"I am familiar enough with Kershian." King vvatha leaned forward. "We have found quarters for the Kershian soldiers and are helping with treatment of the injured. We will make sure the dead are returned respectfully to their families. Of course, this will cost a great deal, not to mention the expense of rebuilding. We would be willing to overlook a portion of this if the Kershians left their airship and battleship as Sombi possessions."

"It was my people who undertook the capture of the ship." Cal rubbed her forehead. "It isn't the best design, though it does have its strengths. I hesitate to give away my people's trophy, but I can agree to train King vvatha's designated people in the process of building an airship from beginning to end."

"Agreed." King vvatha smirked and Cal realized that was his intention from the start.

"King vvatha, the negotiations might not be as much fun, but quicker if you stated what you actually want up front. I'm no politician, so I'm not used to dancing around the issue." Cal sighed.

"I want access to all the knowledge of machinery gained from the Kershians."

"That is not a problem in any area in which I am competent. I know little about firearms and cannons." She leaned on her elbows. "You will also have to accept that you will not have exclusive access to the technology." King vvatha frowned but nodded.

"The battleship was not captured." General Mizvrat said, "there are many sensitive areas I do not want to give away."

"You surrendered to the airship controlled by Congu warriors fighting on the behalf of Sombi. I think keeping it as a prize is reasonable." The king thinned his lips.

"We keep the troop transport ship to take our men home." General Mizvrat met the king's gaze without flinching. "And get to go through the battleship to remove any secret technology."

"I can agree to the troopship, but we must have the battleship intact."

"Listen you two, I'm too tired for this. General Mizvrat, you know who I am and that I was involved in the development of the steam technology on that ship. Whether you destroy it or not, we already possess it."

"We can't risk the information falling into the hands of the Anglians."

Cal laughed bitterly. "I am no longer Anglian. Thanks to your goons, I'm dead and buried there. I will not be sharing secrets with Anglia."

General Mizvrat lowered his head. "I will leave the battleship as is with the understanding that you do not use the ship against Kershia."

"I am not so greedy as to want the world." King vvatha scowled. "It is Kershia who brought their greed here. I have no interest in what Kershia does outside my country. Kershia will recognize the countries of Harasah as sovereign nations and rein in those who have been pillaging the continent for their personal gain. If this is not done quickly enough, we will deal with the problem our way."

"Imagine the access an airship has to destroy fortifications your people think impregnable to Harasahn forces," Cal said.

"You would still have to build an airship—" General Mizvrat sputtered.

"We have an airship, and we have built three of our own." King vvatha growled at him. "You shot looters who disobeyed orders. These are just looters on a larger scale. I am not saying to abandon your presence, but it must be based on trade, not conquest."

"I will speak to the Emperor about the issue. I cannot make such a broad decision on my own."

"You misunderstand." King vvatha said, "Congu, Sombi and others are already sovereign nations. We aren't asking your permission; we are informing you. Traders who break the law of the countries they work in will be brought to justice in our courts."

"What about Anglian interests?"

"What about them? They will work by the same laws as any other country who wishes to do business here."

"I will inform the emperor of your declaration." General Mizvrat shrank into himself.

"Kershia will sign a non-aggression pact with the Harasah Council of Nations." King vvatha crossed his arms.

"We have the right to protect our interests." The general slapped the table.

"Not by military action within the borders of the nations of Harasah. Denial of this item will mean the immediate expulsion of all Kershian company and persons." King vvatha's voice was cold as ice.

"What about the Kershians who are already here?"

"There are no Kershians in this country." King vvatha said. There are Sombi, if some of them have Kershian ancestry that is nothing to us as long as they obey the law. Any who wish to leave will be allowed to."

"They are loyal Kershians with a stake in this —"

"We are holding prisoners who state that they were forced under threat to their families to support the Kershian invasion of Sombi." Cal glared at the general. "We will return them to their communities now that hostilities have ceased." She nodded at King vvatha who shrugged.

"I expected no less from our friends the Congu."

"We will begin transport of the injured who can travel and then the rest of our people. I need assurances that the ones who must wait for the ship to return will be treated properly."

"Do not insult us." King vvatha shouted. "We are not the ones who invaded another country without cause. We are not the savages."

"My apologies, King vvatha." The general looked like a scolded schoolboy.

"I suggest when you speak to the emperor that you suggest he send an ambassador to Harasah, we would be willing to welcome them here in Sombi.

"I can't just go tell the emperor all this. He'll have my head, then come back with a larger force."

"Then your emperor is the problem, and you will have to deal with him. If you try another invasion, then we will have to take action to discipline your country."

The General laughed.

"Don't laugh." Cal made her voice as hard as she could. "The Congu independently developed the airship and the technology to board and take over other airship. We have the technology to destroy whatever navy you send here, and we will be making that technology available to all members of the Harasah Council of Nations. Go speak to your emperor, and if he won't listen, I would suggest you find an emperor who will."

"We can't just replace the Emperor. His heirs would be just as bad."

"Not all of them. I know a young woman who is holding the seal of Kershia and is in line for the throne. You may want to consider supporting her and putting the emperor back under the law of the country."

"She's dead." The General shook his head. "Politics aren't that easy."

"She's not dead, and I didn't say it would be easy, but it is necessary."

"I will return home with the first ship. My second in command will remain here with orders to make sure the Kershians are model visitors in Sombi. The trip will give me some time to consider your suggestions to the emperor." The general stood and bowed to Cal and the king, then left.

Calliope and the Engine Smith

"I think that went rather well." King vvatha also stood. "Go get some rest, you look exhausted."

***

Prince Roger showed up a few days later, arm in a sling.

"I hear you accomplished a number of impossible things."

"A few, yes." Cal hugged him carefully.

"What now?"

"We go back to Kkittu and the cave and start building a university to teach the proper use of technology."

"You don't want to go back to Anglia?"

"That part of my life is done, Roger, and if you ever so much as hint at it again, I will break your other arm."

"I am glad." Roger said, "I would miss you."

***

Svan walked off the troopship, heaving a deep sigh to be back in Kershia. He had mixed feelings. The battle at Biafa was horrible and he was glad to have survived, but many of his friends hadn't, or carried wounds.

"You get a weeks' leave, be sure to report on time." The officer handed a paper to Svan. "Go spend time with your family, it's the best antidote."

"Yes, sir." Svan walked through the crowd at the port and out into the city. A light rain chilled him, but he appreciated it after the heat of Sombi. People who passed him looked the other way; the word of the defeat clearly had become common knowledge.

He thought about stopping into a restaurant, but the idea of interacting with people who might ask about the battle was worse than the slight hunger he felt. Instead, he headed for a hostel. The plain building welcomed him. It wasn't a busy season for the pilgrims, as most preferred to travel in drier weather.

"Welcome, Svan." A man at the desk looked up at Svan. "There is a room available. We have a message here for you." The man slid an envelope across the desk.

Svan opened the envelope and read the brief letter.

I still have your ring. Gretta

He smiled and suddenly the day didn't feel nearly as gloomy.

Chapter 26 A Changing World

Emperor Heodvolt stared at the honour guard.

"What do you mean I must come with you? I'm the emperor, I do as I please."

"The assembly of nobles wishes to ask you some questions about the recent campaign in Sombi."

"How is it my fault that General Mizvrat is so incompetent?" The emperor waved away the honour guard. "Let him answer for his actions. Leave me be."

"Our apologies, but this is not a request, it is an order from the people you serve according to the constitution of Kershia." Two of the guards lifted him to his feet and walked him from the room.

The assembly chamber was packed, and people stood outside the doors craning their necks for a view of the proceedings.

"Out of the way of your emperor." He had decided to be gracious and walk under his own power. They parted for him, and he walked to his throne and placed himself on it. Whatever they wanted, he was still the emperor, and his word was law.

"Emperor Heodvolt, uncle." A young slip of a girl welcomed him with a bow. Then he recognized the Curzm girl. She was supposed to be dead. Clearly, General Mizvrat wasn't the only incompetent person serving him.

"As is allowed by the constitution of Kershia, a majority of the major families and of the minor families have asked me to bring a case to them to judge the competency of your rule."

"And you think you will take my throne? I don't care how many people you have bribed. You can't touch me."

"Since you brought up the question of bribes." Astrid pulled out a sheaf of papers. "You presently owe several million to companies who have substantial interests in Harasah. Perhaps you could explain how their influence led to the invasion of Sombi."

"I invaded that place because the savages massacred our people."

"That is the story given to the media. Does it in truth have nothing to do with the coal, steel and other resources certain Kershian companies wanted to exploit?"

"The Third Prince of Congu, chair of the Harasah Council of Nations was present when this massacre happened. He has written an account for us of the military leaders' plan to depose King vvatha and replace him with a young child. Oddly the exact occurrence as in the Desert Kingdom, whose ambassador has asked us to withdraw from the kingdom to allow the restoration of proper government."

"That has nothing to do with me."

"So you weren't aware that the people you sent to develop Sombi were all shareholders in the same mining company."

"Of course not, why should I care? They invested wisely, is that a problem?" The emperor slumped back on the throne.

"Only when that investment dictates military action, not the wellbeing of Kershia."

"I need those resources to stay ahead of the Anglians."

"Uncle, perhaps you could enlighten us about the last invasion of Kershia which makes the Anglians such a threat?"

"Kershia has never been invaded." The emperor snapped back.

"Thank you. Kershia has never been invaded. However, the Kershian Empire was built by invasions of the countries nearest us, included the attempted taking of Ferandica which the Anglians helped stop more than fifty years ago."

"We have a long and glorious history."

"A history of annexing weaker neighbours, creating the minor houses." Astrid waved a hand. "But we aren't here to debate history. Since you decided to invade Sombi and claim its resources for Kershia, or at least a handful of Kershian companies, explain how you planned the invasion."

"General Mizvrat planned the campaign. I had no part of it."

"So you didn't order General Mizvrat to move forward the date of the attack over his objections?"

The emperor opened and closed his mouth.

"He was taking too long," he finally said.

"Too long by what standard, Uncle? Military conquest is a long drawn-out affair. Our glorious history attests to it taking years, if not decades to properly conclude an invasion."

"We didn't have time."

"Why not?"

"We had to protect our investment."

"You mean the investment of the companies to which you owed millions," Astrid said. "So you didn't take time to mount a proper campaign and moved forward with insufficient preparation resulting in Kershia's defeat. Your 'didn't have time' cost Kershia the lives of more than two hundred soldiers, at least that many wounded, a troop carrier, a battleship, several support craft and three airships, one of which was lost because it was boarded and captured in mid-air. Aside from any question of ethics, you hamstrung your own general because you were in a rush."

"What do you know about it? I was fighting wars before you were born." The emperor jumped up and pointed at her.

"Which war, exactly? You were a baby during the last war, which also failed and cost us millions in reparations." Astrid ignored him and kept pretending to read from the sheaf of papers. "The truth is you thought, because you were emperor, you knew more than the man who did serve in that previous war."

"I've had enough of this nonsense. Guards arrest her and anyone who supports her."

Not one guard so much as twitched.

"You're taking her seriously?" He looked around. "I am the emperor! You obey me."

"Your pardon, sire, but we reviewed the constitution." The head of the Votraiz family stood. "The emperor is to be the servant of the empire."

"That's just words." The emperor shouted.

Calliope and the Engine Smith

"Not just words, the words of the oath you made upon taking the throne. After due consideration, we have decided to take those words seriously. You have done great damage to the reputation and finances of the Kershian Empire. You have clearly demonstrated your incompetence."

"Don't I get a chance to defend myself?"

"You had one. We appointed a representative for you when you refused to attend the meetings you were requested to. They argued quite eloquently in your defence, so much so we decided we needed to hear from your own mouth. You have shown by your own words that you think nothing of the good of our country. You may choose between death or exile."

"How much did my son pay you to do this?"

"Your son has also been deemed inappropriate. The council of houses has agreed on someone who put the welfare of her country over her own. We have done so on the understanding that the Emperor, or Empress in this case, must not stand above the country."

***

Commander Harkness tugged at his collar.

"That is my report, your Highness. The Kershians assumed they had technology and numbers to do what they wanted. Given the resounding defeat handed them by the Sombi and Congu, it will only get more difficult to invade Harasah."

"Thank you, Commander, you have done well." Prince Hubert saluted. "You are dismissed."

After he left, the queen came into the room. "What do you think, Hubert?"

"I think we should be finding an ambassador to go to Harasah. Cracking down on any enterprises whose actions would cause an issue, too."

"We will leave that in your hands." She pulled a sealed envelope from a sleeve. "This is a missive from us to the nations of Congu and Sombi, and the Council of Harasah Nation assuring them we will act within our laws to ensure any of our companies will obey their laws. We expect you to deliver it personally. This," she took out another envelope, "is a letter to Calliope Shillingsworth, thanking her for her service to Anglia and guaranteeing her safety should she ever wish to visit her home. We must admit, it would be politically problematic if she just showed up, but given the situation in Harasah, she must be protected, and we will not exile her."

"And the treasure trove of national secrets Cal holds in her head?"

"We recognize some of the things she has created would be useful if they were exclusive to Anglia, but given the speed of development of the electric engine and its usefulness, perhaps we would be best to allow what Cal has in her mind to belong to the world."

"As you wish." Hubert tucked both envelopes into his jacket. "Any message to Cal you don't want in writing?"

"We wish her happiness in her new home and hope she remains a friend to Anglia." The queen said. "Now, we are amused that the young Tvarliz heir has assumed the throne despite all assumptions. On the way to Sombi, we would like you to stop in and give her our regards. She has done us a great favour and made our peace more likely to last. We expect you will take the Adamant along with the new ambassador and any other council you feel you need."

"So this is very definitely not demonstrating Anglia's military might."

"Demonstrating our commitment to science and exploration."

"I will choose my companions accordingly."

***

"I've been thinking about a new kind of engine." Cal put her feet up, it had been another long day getting the University of Kkittu up and running. She'd made excuses not to go visit some Anglian dignitary in Lusundi this week, though he'd arrived in what had to be the Adamant. Llathia said he seemed nice enough, but she was more interested in talking to the scientists who came with him.

"You mean the electric engine?" kkitatin asked.

"It isn't really new anymore," Roger said, "but it was a good guess."

Kkitatin pouted. "No fair, you already knew."

"Cal talks about engines in her sleep." Roger put a hand on Cal's knee.

"Really?" kkitatin's eyes went wide.

"So I am told, and the source is trustworthy." Cal laughed. "Steam engines burn wood or coal to heat water into steam, then use the steam to move pistons to make the engine move. What if we bypassed the steam and went straight to moving the pistons?"

"I don't get it."

"I'm not sure about it myself, but it will give me something to do when I'm not teaching."

"We did decide to build Cal a new workshop," Roger said.

"I want to help," Kkitatin announced.

"Of course you can."

Cal was interrupted by one of the staff knocking on the door.

"Excuse me, but there is someone here to see you, First Wife, at least I think he meant you."

"Well show him in, and maybe put on some tea and bring some of the fruit left over from supper."

"Cal, you do make it hard for someone to deliver a message." Prince Hubert walked through the door and took a seat. "Nice place you have here."

"Who are you?" kkitatin asked.

"He's an old friend," Cal said before Roger or Hubert could speak up. "I'm sure his mother asked him to drop in."

"I was in the neighbourhood." Hubert grinned. "Anyway, mother sent you this letter and her congratulations. You are welcome to stop in for tea if you are ever in Anglia." He passed over the letter.

Calliope and the Engine Smith

"Thank you, Hubert, let your mother know she is welcome to drop in at any time."

"I will do that," Hubert said as the tea and the fruit arrived. "Now, you mentioned a new kind of engine?

"I did." Cal said, "I'm always going to be an engineer, though I must say it is nice to be working for myself. I'm sure you heard about the Eagles during your visit."

"Some of my companions were most interested in the principles involved."

"I'm hoping to make an engine small enough with enough power to put it on an Eagle. I've been experimenting with different possibilities."

Hubert poured himself a cup of tea.

"I'm all ears."

"It's all about compression. We use a boiler to compress steam, what if instead of compressing the air, we made the air expand? We'd lose the weight of boiler and firebox…"

Other Books by Alex

Series:

Calliope Books

Calliope and the Sea Serpent
Calliope and the Royal Engineers
The Third Prince and the Enemy's Daughter
Calliope and the Kershian Empire

Spruce Bay Books
Wendigo Whispers
Cry of the White Moose
Disputed Rock

The Belandria Tarot
The Devil Reversed
The Regent's Reign
The Empire Unbalanced
The World Widens
The Fury Unleashed

Blue in Kamloops
Tranquille Dark
Columbia Smoke

Caldera
Hero's Call

STAND ALONE BOOKS:

Leedles and the Golden Tree
Generation Gap
The Gods Above
Tales of Light and Dark
Like Mushrooms (poetry and photography)
The Heronmaster
Blood and Sparkles, and other stories
Princess of Boring
By the Book
Sarcasm is My Superpower
Playing on Yggdrasil
The Unenchanted Princess

Read short stories and excerpts from his novels at alexmcgilvery.com